PUFFIN BOOKS

Editor: Kaye Webb

PROFESSOR BRANESTAWM'S
TREASURE HUNT

When it was a case of inventing an unspillable teacup, or a collapsible-cum-expandable house, or a liquid carpet to be applied with a brush, or a machine for peeling and pipping grapes, a bomb or a fire alarm, Professor Branestawm was the man for the job. His interests were wide, and his intentions excellent, but it simply isn't any joke to be an inventor, or to be anywhere near one, as the Professor's military friend Colonel Dedshott and his long-suffering housekeeper Mrs Flitter-snoop well knew.

Puffin readers first met this eccentric genius in *The Incredible Adventures of Professor Branestawm*, and they will find the new adventures in this book just as hilariously impossible.

This marvellously funny book is for nine- to twelve-year-olds, particularly boys.

NORMAN HUNTER

PROFESSOR BRANESTAWM'S TREASURE HUNT

and other incredible adventures

Illustrated by George Adamson

PUFFIN BOOKS
IN ASSOCIATION WITH THE BODLEY HEAD

Puffin Books: a Division of Penguin Books Ltd
Harmondsworth, Middlesex, England
Penguin Books Inc, 7110 Ambassador Road, Baltimore, Maryland 21207, U.S.A.
Penguin Books Australia Ltd, Ringwood, Victoria, Australia

—

First published by The Bodley Head 1937
Published in Puffin Books 1966
Reprinted 1967, 1969, 1971, 1973

—

—

Made and Printed in Great Britain
by Hazell Watson & Viney Ltd,
Aylesbury, Bucks
Set in Linotype Baskerville

Contents

The Professor's Treasure Hunt

CARRIER men arrived at the Professor's house one morning with no end of a big and generously wrapped up package.

'Name of Branestawm?' they said, staggered in with the package, and drew out sheets and sheets of forms to be signed here and checked there.

'Oh, ah, thank you, put it here,' said the Professor, flinging open the door of his study and catching Mrs Flittersnoop, his housekeeper, rather a daisy one because she was just inside, polishing the floor.

'Ah, most instructive,' said the Professor, looking at the carrier men through various pairs and sets of pairs of spectacles, as they bonked and rattled and squerked the package through the almost too small doorway and set it down with a thump that shook the calendar a week fast.

'Give them twopence each, will you,' said the Professor to Mrs Flittersnoop, and he immediately began undoing the package; while some slight arguments began outside the door about the twopences because the package had come a sort of C.O.D. way and there was something pounds how many shillings and what pence to pay, which made twopence each look a bit insufficient.

'Excuse me, sir, I'm sure,' began Mrs Flittersnoop, going back to the study for more money. Then she threw up her hands and began to wonder if it was time

to go on another visit to her sister Aggie at Lower Pagwell. For the Professor had got the package almost completely undone from the string and paper and canvas and labels and had got himself rather more than completely wrapped and tangled and tied and fastened up in them instead.

Fortunately at that moment Colonel Dedshott of the Catapult Cavaliers called on the Professor to see if he had any new inventions to make his head go round and round, as the Professor's inventions always did when he listened to descriptions of them. And fortunately too the Colonel had just drawn rather a packet of money out of the bank to buy a new sideboard and had thought he'd better have a bit more than the sideboard cost in case he felt like having a good time.

'Ha, Branestawm, new invention, what!' said the Colonel a bit heartily, after he had paid the what pounds something shillings and how pence, and given the men a shilling each, which pleased them so much they changed hats on the way out which wasn't allowed by the carrier company. 'Automatic parcel-making machine or new kind of clothes?' asked the Colonel.

'No, no, get me out of this – oh dear, I don't understand parcels,' spluttered the Professor mufflishly from inside the wrappings. So the Colonel grabbed at the paper, which collapsed flat and let him down with a crackly wallop because the Professor had felt tired and sat down inside the wrappings.

At last they were more or less sorted out, and the pieces of paper and bits of string and labels were either thrown in the dustbin or folded up and put away in the cupboard on the next shelf to the soap, according to whether Mrs Flittersnoop thought they were nice-looking pieces of paper or lovely bits of string or not. And the Professor and Colonel began looking at a rather exciting old chest with brass corners, which had been inside the parcel.

'Bought it at a sale at Old Pagwell Manor House,' said the Professor, cramming all his five pairs of spectacles into various pockets and hopping inside the chest to see what was what, if anything was.

'Ha,' grunted the Colonel, who didn't think much

of old chests, but he wanted to be polite, so he stooped down to look at one of the brass corners. It immediately shot out and hit him in his own chest, which made rather a din, what with all the Colonel's medals and the brass corner and what the Colonel said, which was nothing much in words but plentifully much in sounds.

'Good gracious, even more instructive than I hoped,' said the Professor, coming out of the chest again and tugging handfuls of spectacles out of every pocket. 'Why, it's a secret compartment, similar in construction to those sometimes found in old Spandaluvian state chests and believed to exist in some of the more remotely western of the native boogle dwellings of Inner Outwaze.'

'It hit me in the chest,' grunted the Colonel, dusting himself down rather jinglingly among his medals.

Then both he and the Professor suddenly craned their necks forward and peered into the secret drawer, taking no notice of the fact that they bumped their heads together through the Professor's neck craning further than either of them expected. Because there in the drawer was a roll of yellow sort of paper, musty and definitely smelly but most sensationally interesting looking.

'A chart,' gasped the Professor, getting the paper out of the chest and spread on the floor with himself spread all over it and his spectacles spread all round. 'Dear, dear, most astounding. It shows where to find hidden treasure.'

'Where?' cried the Colonel, coming down flop beside the Professor and putting on the Professor's look-at-you-over-the-top-of spectacles in the excitement and on top of his own eyeglass, which made him look

rather rum but made the chart look still more rum to him because everything went all wavy.

'It's all quite clear, bless me,' chattered the Professor, following red lines and going off at tangents and noticing compass points.

'We must fit out expedition,' cried the Colonel, springing to his feet. 'Here is money I was going to buy sideboard with, what! Sideboards can wait. How do we begin and when do we start? Come on Branestawm; my word, you know, treasure and adventure and all that. We'll be rich!' He grabbed the Professor with one hand and the chart with the other, and shot out of the house to see about fitting out an expedition without stopping to think how one set about it. And Mrs Flitter-snoop, coming into the study two seconds later to ask if the Colonel was staying to dinner and if so how was she going to manage as there was only one chop, found she could manage very well by having the chop herself.

The Branestawm-Dedshott Treasure Hunting Expedition was on its way to the island shown on the chart. Colonel Dedshott had found a stepbrother of a once-was Catapult Cavalier who knew a man who had a barge sort of boat on the East Pagwell Canal. So they got him to be captain of the ship which Professor Branestawm managed, goodness knows how, to get the Pagwell Deep Sea Fisheries and Inland Waterways Repair Council to lend him. It wasn't much of a ship as liners go, being only so many whatsnames long and having a thingummybob of less than such and such how-d'ye-call-'ems.

But all the same, it was none too skinny a ship if you had to row it with oars, which thank goodness you hadn't to, as the inside part was plentifully full of engines and things, and funnels grew out of its back, and there was a bridge with little levers to pull and make bells go ting-ting and the engines go chug-a-chug and the propeller arrangements go swoosh-a-woosh and all the rest of that seafaring stuff.

'Well, it'll be a nice holiday for us, I'm sure, sir, even if we don't find the treasure,' said Mrs Flitter-snoop, who had come as ship's cook. 'Not that I hold with findings beings keepings, as you might say.' Then she went down into a cabin to see about getting cups of tea but was seasick before she could get them. Then Colonel Dedshott was seasick, tried not to show it, but didn't come anywhere near succeeding.

Professor Branestawm went up on the bridge to see if steering ships looked interesting and found it looked most puzzling, partly because the captain was driving the ship backwards, not thinking it mattered which end went first, as he was used to barge and lighter sort of boats which are made the same both ends like trams only a bit different.

'When do we get there?' asked the Professor, trying to tell the time by some sort of instrument that had something to do with latitudes.

The captain didn't answer. He was seasick too, because the sea was so much more unsteady than Pagwell Canal, and what with the ship going backwards, and there not being any cups of anything through Mrs Flittersnoop having lost interest in being ship's cook, he didn't feel so nautical as he'd expected.

'Um, dear me,' said the Professor, grabbing the wheel not quite in time to prevent the ship turning right round and beginning to go properly forwards. 'This treasure hunting business is most worrying. There's so much sea about one can't tell whether one is going the right way. I wonder if I could invent something to . . .' Then the Professor was seasick and the ship went round in circles until the following Tuesday teatime, when thank goodness everyone felt all right again and cups of things were got going. Mrs Flittersnoop started being ship's cook ever so much more successfully than she'd expected because everything was in tins and getting breakfast, lunch, dinner, tea or supper was just a matter of: Tin open, tin empty, plates full, tummies full, plates empty, and then wash up; the last part being the easiest of all because you had only to trail them over the side and let the sea do the work, which it didn't seem to mind doing, only once a fish got one of the best teacups, though fortunately it was the cracked one.

'Land ho!' shouted the man up in the look-out. He was a fireman friend of Mrs Flittersnoop's from the Pagwell Fire Station, and he'd shouted 'Land ho!' six times a day, all of which so far had turned out to be either schools of porpoises or single whales or clumps of seaweed or specks of dirt on the glass of the telescope. But this time it was the real thing, and the ship ran aground before the captain could make up his mind what he ought to do.

'Well, well, welcome to the island,' cried Colonel Dedshott, jumping off the ship in a nice white uniform and landing no end of a slodge in some exceedingly puddingy sand, from which it took the entire crew half an hour to pull him out, even with the help of the thing for hauling up the anchor with.

At last they all got themselves on to the island, but not before the Professor had studied the chart and found it was the wrong island; then found he was looking at it the wrong way round and that it was the right one after all, and then seen a little squiggle which upset his calculation and proved it definitely was the wrong one, and finally having discovered that the squiggle was a tea leaf, which evened things up and made it the right island, thank goodness.

'Captain must stay on board with two men,' cried Colonel Dedshott, who had changed his trousers and was beginning to feel like old times again, commanding people about. Then off they set to search for the treasure, but had to stop about four times every yard to persuade Professor Branestawm to come away from some new kind of starfish or some unheard-of sort of plant or some unexpected variety of rock, which the island seemed to be full of, perhaps to make things harder.

'Turn left, right here,' cried the Colonel as they filed through a cleft in some rocks, 'then into this sandy cove.'

'There's another cove up in that tree, a black one,' said the fireman, who had been look-out and got used to being sharp with his eyes, though he was a bit funny with his tongue.

'Good gracious!' cried the Professor. 'Why, that looks like a member of the Bangsloshly tribe of Diddituptites, a fierce race of cannibals if I remember rightly.'

The Professor certainly did remember rightly for once, for the black gentleman up in the tree let out a noise like an entire Sunday's washing-up going down the drain and immediately the scenery was full of more black gentlemen making similar noises and waving no end of assorted cutlery.

Colonel Dedshott instantly let fly with his catapult at the biggest native but missed him and knocked two striped parrots off a bush. The big black person flung a handful of spears in the Colonel's direction. The Colonel ducked, but he needn't have bothered because the spears all fell short, and while the big black person was collecting them all again for another go, the rest of the natives gathered round and started shushing the Colonel, the Professor, Mrs Flittersnoop and the rest of them along to where they lived.

'I don't know whether to wish I hadn't come on this expedition because it looks like being dangerous,' murmured the Professor, 'or whether to be glad I have because it looks like being interesting. I wonder if I can remember the sort of language these people talk, and if I can, what difference will it make if any.' He had a few thinks as they went along and had managed to remember quite a number of native words, one which meant 'notwithstanding', one which meant either 'kill me' or else meant 'I'm hungry,' he couldn't be sure which, and one which meant 'oo-er' and was the same in any language, being more of a gurgle than a word, which was what most of the native words were anyway, possibly to make them easier to say with your mouth full as the natives didn't go in much for manners.

'Tight corner,' whispered Colonel Dedshott out of one corner of his mouth to make it seem secret. 'Must get message to men on ship. Rescue and all that, what!'

'I did know some native words that meant "who has seen the garden roller of the policeman's mother?" ' said the Professor, 'but I'm afraid if I remembered them they wouldn't be much use.'

'Pah,' whispered the Colonel, but found it rather a difficult thing to whisper, 'this is danger. They may be cannibals. May eat us. Most disagreeable. How can we get rescued?'

'Oh dear, I'm sure I wish I'd never come,' wailed Mrs Flittersnoop. 'I might have known no good would come of looking for treasure that belongs to someone else, though perhaps they did come by it dishonestly as you might say. Oh, I wish I was sitting by the gas cooker in the kitchen again, that I do, and never mind what the Professor invented, the poor gentleman.'

By that time they all found themselves sitting uncomfortably near to a decidedly un-gas cooker. In fact they had reached the native village and were in a clearing surrounded by huts shaped like candle extinguishers because that was the easiest shape to make and made of goodness knows what, which was probably the easiest way to make them. And in the centre of the clearing was an unreasonably large fire for so warm a day and hanging over the fire was an unpleasantly large-looking pot.

'Um – er – as I feared,' muttered the Professor, as he and Colonel Dedshott and Mrs Flittersnoop sat round the big pot hanging over the enormous fire, where the Diddituptite natives had brought them. 'I always maintained that this type of native was cannibal, though my book on the subject never received the consideration it deserved. Most gratifying to know that I was right after all, but I don't like this being eaten idea at all when it comes to realities.'

Suddenly there was a loud howl like all the cats in Lower Pagwell being trodden on at once, and into the clearing leapt three black gentlemen dressed in quantities of coloured paint, and having their faces painted to look as if they had them on upside down.

'Bless me, why they're going to do the Diddituptite feast dance,' said the Professor, ' a thing I have heard of but never seen. This will be most exceptionally interesting. I shall have to write a book about it.'

The dance began. The three black gentlemen stood on their heads. Then they stood on each other's heads. They ran round in circles backwards. They rubbed their noses on the ground.

'Close up a bit,' whispered the Colonel very urgently. 'Have got idea. Will slip silently away while everyone looking at dance. Fetch help. Get them not to eat you till I get back. Good luck to me, what!'

The Colonel sank slowly to the ground and wriggled away through the long grass while Mrs Flittersnoop closed up against the fireman look-out man. But the

Professor was too interested to do any closing up. Instead he gave a shout that was meant to sound like several cats being trodden on at once, but which sounded more like one cat being trodden on several times. Then he stood on his head. He ran round in circles backwards. He rubbed his hands on the ground. He rubbed his nose on the ground and all his pairs of spectacles fell off. He had remembered that he knew all about the Diddituptite feast dance and thought it might not do any harm if he joined in.

Gasps went up from the natives. The three upside-down-face gentlemen stopped in the very act of banging each other's heads together and gaped at the Professor as he tried to stand on his own tummy.

'There now, I knew he ought to have brought his straw hat in case of the sun,' wailed Mrs Flittersnoop.

The Professor solemnly bowed to the upside-down-face gentlemen and began to hop along on one foot while he tried to put the other one in his mouth, but didn't come very near succeeding.

More yells and gasps went up. The three upside-down-face gentlemen bowed and hopped and put their feet so successfully in their mouths they nearly swallowed themselves, which wasn't the idea at all even though they were cannibals. The dance went on. The shouts and howls went up. The fire went out because the Professor bumped accidentally against the pot and tipped the water out. Then the Professor and the upside-down-face people lay flat on their backs and kicked their heels in the air, which was the finish of the dance.

The howls died away and an extra large and highly decorated person wearing positively necklaces of teeth and a hat made of four condensed milk tins tied

together with red grass strode forward and stood the
Professor right way up.

'Oh mighty white man, who knows all about our
amazing dance! Welcome to Bangsloshly! Welcome!'
he cried in his own language which the Professor was
none to sure if he understood, though he could speak
small portions of it.

'Who has seen the garden roller of the policeman's
mother?' said the Professor, getting out the first native
words he could think of, which were the ones he had
just remembered.

'Ha, ha, ha, the great white chief is graciously
pleased to make the joke,' roared the black chief still
in his own language as he didn't know any other. He

clapped the Professor heartily on the back in any language and all his pairs of spectacles flew off again in a shower.

'Oh mighty white chief, who can take off his eyes,' cried the black chief, 'you and your friends must remain for a stop with us.'

'Notwithstanding,' said the Professor, remembering another word.

'Notwithstanding it shall be,' shouted the chief. 'Come let us sit,' and everyone instantly sat down, a good many of them on top of each other though they didn't seem to mind being in layers; while Mrs Flittersnoop, who was good at picnics, made herself very nearly comfortable on what looked like a bit of soft ground but was really an ants' nest, but thank goodness a disused one.

Then the Professor and the chief began having another try at talking, and whether it was hearing so much of the language or whether it was that the dance had improved his memory, the Professor began to remember large slabs of Diddituptite conversation. He introduced Mrs Flittersnoop, who stood up to curtsey and fell over again doing it. He introduced the look-out fireman, who touched his forehead and said 'How do'. He introduced Colonel Dedshott, found he wasn't there and managed to stop the introduction halfway through and turn it into a polite question as to how the wife of the black chief was. The Didditup-tite language was rather convenient in that way.

Then cups of something hot that looked like tea, smelt like coffee, and tasted like cocoa made from pork gravy were handed round and the Professor began explaining about the treasure hunt with the help of the chart arrangement. Everything looked as if it was going to be all lovely after all. They weren't going to be eaten. They were probably going to be helped to find the treasure. Hurray and everything!

Colonel Dedshott, as he slipped and sidled and slank through the long thin waving wiggly grass to get some rescue, knowing nothing of the Professor making friends with the natives, was all of several dithers. One in case he should be captured before he got anywhere much. One in case he couldn't find anywhere much to get. One in case he couldn't get any rescue and one in case he got back with the rescue too late. But he needn't have worried. He wasn't caught; he got somewhere, he got back to where they'd left the ship. But the ship wasn't there! The captain and the rest of those on board had got tired of waiting. They'd managed to push the ship off the sand into deep water again, chiefly with the help of some definitely sloshy waves which would have got it back anyway, and now they were fishing happily for whales, thank goodness without catching any, as even one none-too-large whale could have batted the ship clean back to Pagwell Docks with one wallop of its tail or whatever it is that whales wallop ships with, which they probably do when caught.

'Ahoy,' cried the Colonel in a whisper so that the natives shouldn't hear. But the captain didn't hear either, so he waved his hat. The captain was looking the other way. He waved his shirt and the captain saw it but only waved back, thinking he was being friendly. 'Ha,' grunted Colonel Dedshott, and he swam out to the ship, spoiling his second pair of trousers in one day. But what were trousers when the Professor was in danger of being eaten? What indeed! Though as he wasn't in danger everything was slightly silly, but how was the Colonel to know? Anyway he had plenty more trousers at home.

'Professor captured by cannibals,' he spluttered, crawling on board at last. 'Full steam, find gunboats or soldier ships or something. Urgent, hurry, ha, what!'

The captain was a bit slow on the uptake where this sort of thing was concerned, but after a bit of a time and plenty of hand waving, and talking round corners at each other, he grasped the Colonel's meaning and off shot the ship in the direction of what they hoped might be some sort of rescue, and by some sort of amazing luck, possibly because it was Friday the thirteenth, or because the latitude divided into the longitude with none over, they almost immediately met a cruiser sort of battleship positively oozing with guns and literally overrun with sailors, which was going round to see that nothing nasty was done by anyone to someone.

Of course the commander of the cruiser was as quick as lightning on the uptake about cannibals, and was soon anchored off the island and packing sailors into boats by the dozen for rowing to the shore.

'Hurray, rescue, good old Branestawm,' sang out the Colonel, who had put a naval sort of hat on and was trying to be the same thing on the sea as a colonel is on land only more so if anything. He sprang into the last boat, missed it and spoilt a third pair of trousers, but got to the island by hanging on to the rudder of the boat.

On the island Professor Branestawm and the black gentlemen had got along so well together that they'd managed to reckon where the treasure was supposed to be hidden and get themselves all there with no end of pickaxes and shovels and rows of buckets, some of them native ones made from bazonka-bazinka leaves, rather pretty but not the remotest bit watertight, which didn't matter as it was treasure they hoped to fill them with.

'This is the spot,' said the chief, still in his own language. He shouted orders and the natives began digging holes like anything but didn't get on too fast to begin with, because the earth that one lot were throwing out of their hole was falling into the hole that another lot were trying to dig. But it didn't seem to matter much because after rather a time of it they had so many holes dug all over the place shown on the chart that it looked like a sort of enormous thing for holding terrific eggs. In fact, just as they had the last hole dug an Izitwatt or Zam Zam bird flew by and laid a mighty egg in it without stopping, which caused plentiful commotion, because the egg burst and a whole flock of young Izitwatts flew out in a shower like so many sparrows only there were more of them.

'Funny business this treasure hunting,' said the Professor, looking at the chart through his near-sighted glasses and not seeing the Izitwatts, which was a pity in one way, because he would have liked to see them, but was a good job in another way, because he would probably have run after them to try to catch one, and lost himself as well as all interest in the treasure. 'Can't understand this chart arrangement. We've dug holes all over where it says, but there's no treasure. Can it be a hoax and if so, why? Bless me, most distracting.'

'Do you think, sir, begging your pardon for making so bold, sir, I'm sure,' said Mrs Flittersnoop, who was getting so tired of treasure hunts and black gentlemen and feast dances, that she would have gone back to her sister Aggie in Lower Pagwell if it hadn't been so far, 'I mean to say, sir, perhaps the treasure is somewhere else, and they only put that paper in the chest to mislead you like, so to speak.'

'Um, yes, I didn't think of that,' said the Professor. 'Er—um, most annoying. It ought to be stopped. Ah! but wait a moment; if they wanted to mislead us, why did they put any charts anywhere or say anything about any treasure? No, no, the treasure must be here somewhere. We probably took the wrong number of paces in not the right direction from a different tree than was intended.'

'Yes, sir, I'm sure, if you say so,' said Mrs Flittersnoop. But it was hardly likely, for the chart didn't show any trees and said nothing about steps being taken in any direction.'

The Professor took off his hat to scratch his head and a large but happily harmless spider came zim zim down from a craggy piece of rock above and scratched it for him.

'Ow! Oh – er – um, go away, do,' cried the Professor, jumping back and looking up at the spider, which he recognized as some kind of a one he knew all about, so wasn't much interested, when he suddenly gave quite different sorts of exclamations. For up among the rocks he could see the corner of what looked like a box sticking out of where some of the rock had fallen away.

'The treasure!' he yelled, forgetting to speak the native language, but as he pointed up it didn't matter.

'Amazing,' said the chief, but it didn't sound much like it in his talk.

'No wonder we couldn't find it by digging holes,' said the Professor. 'We must have been looking at the chart upside down. Silly of us. But why didn't they put "top" at the top of the chart? Most careless.'

By this time the chief had got his men at it again,

climbing on top of each other to make a sort of human ladder, then up the ladder he went his own chief self, but as he was on the large side, the whole lot collapsed when he was five-eighths of the way up, and the ladder took some putting together again as some of the members of it had fallen into the holes they had dug and were finding them on the dozy side. At last with plenty of shouting, the human ladder was again raised, and this time the fireman look-out, who was used to ladders even if they were red ones instead of black ones, clambered up and managed to get the box out of the rocky niche.

'Hurray!' yelled the Professor.

'Rescue! Good old Branestawm, here we come,' yelled another voice, and through the bushes burst Colonel Dedshott with his trousers still unchanged, and followed by clumps of sailors with rifles.

Bang! bang! ta-rattety bang! went the rifles, but the sailors were firing into the air to scare the natives.

'No, no, no, no!' screamed Professor Branestawm, waving his hands, one of them full of five pairs of spectacles, while the safety pins which fastened his coat in place of the buttons that had fallen off, burst off in all directions.

'Ya, ya, wow, ow, ya, ya, zazza, bom!' roared the natives, and they would have flung spears, not up in the air but at the sailors, only they'd left their spears at home.

'Rescue!' roared Colonel Dedshott, letting fly with his catapult, but hitting a rather important sailor somewhere unimportant instead.

Consternation began to reign. Shouts and rifles and a catapult were let off all round. The chief native threw a rock. It missed everyone, but dropped thunderishly wallop on to the treasure chest, which split like a banana only different. Everyone made a dash for the chest. Nearly everyone got tangled up in someone else. The Professor got tangled up in himself, which was more than enough. Mrs Flittersnoop hid behind what she thought was a bush but it was a grass sort of robe the chief native wore, and he moved away to get another rock, leaving her all exposed, which she didn't know as she had her face down one of the treasure holes.

Oh dreadful thing! Oh that rescue should have come just when it wasn't wanted! Oh what would the natives think? What would they do? The upside-down-faced men might start their dance again. Everything might be awful.

Natives and soldiers were struggling over bags of gold in the treasure box. Colonel Dedshott and Professor Branestawm were struggling, the Colonel to shake the Professor's hand and the Professor to explain everything at once, but he had such a rush of words to the mouth he couldn't say any of them. At last, with a most indigestible gulp, which gave him an interesting but unpleasant kind of pain, he managed to stammer out, 'No, no, natives friends, I knew dance, they helped find treasure, yes, no, stop, oh my goodness, puff, puff!'

'What!' gasped the Colonel, letting go of the Professor, who fell over, as he was hanging on to the Colonel a bit heavily. 'Natives friends! Helped find what, who, hey! Oh, as-you-were, cease fire, whoa!' He dashed round the tangle of natives and sailors, and gradually, with the help of the Professor who gabbled no end of native talk, managed to get things explained and sorted out.

'You must share the treasure,' said the Professor to the native chief as they sat round the fire in the native village, having a sort of a kind of a dinner of a sort of a rice and some kind of carrots. He laid his spectacles on the side of his plate and Mrs Flittersnoop, who was giving a hand with the serving, helped him to rather a slosh of rice right on top of them because she was looking to see if anyone else wanted some more.

'No, no,' said the chief. 'Treasure no good. Gold not understand. Nothing to buy here. Give me those eyes that go off and on and all is well.' He scooped the rice off the Professor's plate and put the spectacles on upside down with rice still sticking to them.

'But I – er – that is,' began the Professor. But it was no use. He had to give the chief all his five pairs of spectacles and make elaborate notes to get five more pairs when he got back to Pagwell. But, hurrah! there was generously much treasure to spare even after they'd shared round a bit to the sailors. So when the Professor, the Colonel, Mrs Flittersnoop and the others got back to Pagwell, the Professor was able not only to have five more pairs of spectacles and an entirely new set of safety pins for his coat, but also to build a new and extensively big Inventory, while the Colonel bought himself eighteen more pairs of trousers to make up for those he'd spoilt in the sea, and Mrs Flittersnoop, who had wanted to take home a butter dish with 'A present from Bangsloshly' on it, but of course couldn't get one, took her sister Aggie a new feather boa so that she could borrow it on Sundays, and bought herself a new hat which suited her twice as well as her old one, which was not at all.

2

The Great Invisibleness

JINGLING and clattering sounds echoed rather noisily through the streets of Great Pagwell. Brisk tap-tap-tappety-taps resounded on the hard, pink pavements, which had the words 'Pagwell Council' stamped in brass every few yards, possibly in case anyone thought the pavements belonged to anyone who cared to chip off a bit to make a rockery with, but more likely to let the Pagwell Council show off a bit, which was almost the only thing it did about which all its members agreed.

Tingle-jingle. Rap-tap-tap. Were roads getting ready to be up? Was there to be no thoroughfare somewhere? Had one to beware of the steam-roller and were cyclists advised to walk? No, no, nothing of the kind. It was Colonel Dedshott of the Catapult Cavaliers, out for what was his idea of a morning stroll, but which was definitely more like most people's idea of a very energetic and bashy kind of physical jerks, to be done to make one's muscles larger, or one's waist smaller, according to whether one was a lady or a gentleman.

Suddenly the jingling, which was the Colonel's many medals leaping about on his chest, stopped, and the rap-tapping, which was the Colonel's drastically military heels hitting the pavement, broke off, as if he had either been snatched up into the sky by an unexpected balloon, or dropped through the earth by an unseen coal-hole.

'Ha, my word, etcetera,' grunted the Colonel, for he was neither in the air nor down a coal-hole, but simply somewhat motionless on the kerb. 'Branestawm, or I'm a Dutchman, you know, what!'

Well, of course the Colonel wasn't a Dutchman, though it would have made no difference if he had been. It definitely was Professor Branestawm that he had seen. And the Professor was striding silently along on the other side of the road, his head bent down, and not looking where he was going. Perhaps that was because he hadn't made up his mind where he was going.

Anyway, with grunts of joy the Colonel, who hadn't seen Professor Branestawm for rather a wedge of a time, shot briskly and janglingly across the Pagwell Council's nice, tidy road, two inches in front of a nervous lady cyclist out for the first time, who twiddled her front wheel exceedingly too much, and slid comparatively gracefully, into a deep wire Pagwell Council waste-paper basket, intended to hold almost anything from bun bags to orange-peel, but probably not nervous lady cyclists.

'Ha, hullo, Branestawm, thinking again, what?' cried the Colonel, and he clapped the Professor on the shoulder. At least, he thought he was going to clap the Professor on the shoulder. But good gracious him and all! Something stopped him! Yes, yes, most amazing and unbelievable thing, a sort of an invisible something or other stopped the Colonel's hand in mid-air!

'Hm,' grunted the Colonel, not believing it. He had another go. Again the invisible something stopped him. He ran after the Professor and made a grab at him. Heavens! A cold, hard, invisible nothing at all struck him in the face.

By this time the Colonel's blood was up. Was he, a Dedshott of the Dedshotts, a Colonel of the Catapult Cavaliers, an R.S.V.P., a P.I.P., not to mention a life member of the Pagwell District Calceolaria Society – was he to be daunted by invisible nothings, and kept from greeting his old friend? Not he! Daunting wasn't in the Colonel's line, at least not so far as being it was concerned, though doing it to other people was another matter.

He raced after the Professor, but the Professor didn't see him. He shouted the Professor's name, but the Professor didn't hear him. He hurled himself repeatedly and energetically at the Professor, but bounced off nothing he could see before he reached him.

At last the Colonel lost the Professor in a crowd through which he walked like a hot knife going through butter, with people bouncing away from him in all directions without seeming to know why.

'Hm, strange, don't understand it, what!' said the Colonel, blowing through his whiskers till they stood out straight from his face. 'Must go and see Branestawm this evening, ha, yes.'

Professor Branestawm was just sitting down to supper when the Colonel arrived. But it looked the most unlikely sort of supper, even for the Professor, who was a bit given to having unlikely meals.

There were quantities of stewed fruit and custard standing about all by themselves, not in bowls or dishes, but just standing sort of shaped up all on their own. There was a jug of lemonade without any jug round it, and no glasses to drink out of. Some flowers floated gracefully all by themselves several inches above the table, while in one corner of the room Mrs Flittersnoop's own favourite goldfish swam happily about, in a large globe-shaped portion of water contained in nothing at all. It was most weird.

'My dear Dedshott,' said the Professor, jumping up and kicking his chair over backwards, 'this is delightful, really, my dear fellow; you are just in time to witness one of the most remarkable successes it has ever been my fortune to – er – to – to – er – that is to –'

'To whatsname thingummy, what, Branestawm,' roared the Colonel, clapping the Professor heartily on the shoulder, so that he sat down suddenly on the knocked over chair, and got himself wedged between the front legs, which were sticking out like arms.

Then in came Mrs Flittersnoop, with an armful of chicken broth in no bowl. The Professor struggled out of the wrong-way-up chair, and the sensational supper began.

'Lemonade, Dedshott?' said the Professor. He picked up the lemonade, poured some of it out into the air, where it stayed in a little lump, which the Professor put in front of the Colonel. Then he ladled some broth out into a flat sort of disc and handed it to the Colonel, who took it very gingerly, and found there was a plate round it that he couldn't see.

'Ah ha, Dedshott, what do you think of that?' chuckled the Professor, scooping one of his five pairs of spectacles out of the broth where they had fallen, and hanging them on the flowers to dry. 'That is rather a surprise I fancy, is it not?'

'Amazing, incredible, my word, Branestawm; what is it, you know, hey?' gasped the Colonel.

'Branestawm's non-shine glass,' said the Professor, with the air of a man showing people over ancient ruins. 'Now glass, as you know,' he went on, leaning

forward so rapidly that all his remaining four pairs of glasses slid with several splashes into his lemonade, 'glass can be seen through, so it ought to be invisible. But it is not invisible. You can see a window. You can see a glass jug. Why?'

'Marvellous,' muttered the Colonel, with his mouth

full of broth and lemonade, mixed, which didn't mix too well.

'You can see them because they shine. They reflect the light. But supposing they were transparent and did not reflect the light? You wouldn't be able to see them. They would be invisible.'

'Hurray,' said the Colonel, who hadn't been listening much, because he knew the Professor's description would make his head go round and round, and he'd just had his hair washed, so preferred it to stay still.

'I have invented a new kind of glass,' said the Professor, 'glass that does not shine. Glass that is invisible. These dishes and tumblers are made from it;' he waved his hand round the table and knocked the lemonade all over the custard.

The Colonel dropped his spoon with a clatter.

'I saw you this afternoon, but couldn't get near you,' he said. 'Something invisible surrounded you. That wasn't glass, what?'

'Yes, yes,' cried the Professor, waving his other hand, but waving it more carefully. 'I made a big glass shade of my invisible glass, and went out in it. Caused quite a sensation. There will be something in the newspapers about it.'

'Hm,' said the Colonel, who hardly ever read newspapers, but only wrote letters to them. 'Well, what are you going to do with your invention?'

'That is just my trouble, Dedshott,' said the Professor, putting all his glasses on in a clump. 'The invention is marvellous, though I say it myself. It will revolutionize our ideas about glass. Nothing like it has ever been invented before. It is invisibility discovered. But I must admit – er – Dedshott, that I have really no idea what use it is. Except,' he added, 'that one can have a little harmless amusement with it, such as we are having at this moment.' He ladled some rhubarb on to what he thought was the Colonel's plate, but the Colonel wasn't holding a plate and the rhubarb went up his sleeve.

'Pah,' spluttered the Colonel, not thinking too much of the Professor's idea of harmless amusement. Then he had an idea, and said so.

'Excellent,' said the Professor. As a rule he didn't see what Colonel sort of people wanted to go having ideas for, but this time it looked like being possibly of some use, though probably not much.

'Shop windows, you know,' said the Colonel. 'The glass shines in your eyes. Can't see the things in the window properly, and all that, especially on sunny days. Non-shine glass just the thing.'

'I – er – but that is –' began the Professor, but the Colonel couldn't stop.

'Friend of mine owns Great Pagwell Furnishing Company,' he shouted excitedly, shaking rhubarb about in pink showers. 'Bring a piece of your glass, I will introduce you. If he uses it for windows in his shop, it will mean a good thing for you, Branestawm, what! My word, yes. Fine idea. Come round with me to-morrow.'

Next morning Colonel Dedshott was up bright and early, and called for the Professor. But he'd forgotten all about the Pagwell Furnishing Company, and was doing a bit of before-breakfast inventing, sitting up in bed, with hammers and things all over the eiderdown.

'Really, Branestawm, you are most – er – most – ha –

hum – yes, my word, you are, you know. Now I shall have to wait while you dress.'

But that was where he was wrong, for the Professor was already dressed under his pyjamas, except for his back collar-stud, and soon they were on their way to the Pagwell Furnishing Company, while Mrs Flittersnoop was having the most unmentionable time of it, trying to wash up the invisible supper things, and having bits of them come off in her hand without knowing it.

By the time the Professor and the Colonel arrived at the Pagwell Furnishing Store it was still bright, but no longer early, because they'd had to stop several times on the way: once for the Professor to change his boots over, as he had them on the wrong feet ; four times to get him away from steam-rollers, road-up drills, traction engines, and an ice-cream cart, which had given him ideas for might-possibly-be inventions ; twice for the Colonel to say 'Good morning' to some friends, who seemed to have rather long-drawn-out ideas of saying 'Good morning'; and once for the Professor to say 'Good morning' to a friend of his who turned out not to be a friend at all, but someone who looked like Mrs Flittersnoop's cousin's young man when seen through the long-sighted glasses that the Professor was looking through, and who was really a Chinese gentleman come to Pagwell to study basket-work, and needed no end of a lot of explaining to before they could get away.

'Ah, here we are at last,' cried the Colonel, as they reached a huge building, composed mainly of windows and gold lettering. The Colonel pushed open the big swing doors, and went in, followed by the Professor, who wasn't thinking of swing doors, and they swung back and batted him rather firmly out on to the pavement again, where he sat in a little tin marked 'Drink, puppy, drink,' rather to the surprise of a very weeny puppy, who couldn't make up his mind how he was to drink anything like the Professor.

By the time the Professor had got away from the puppy, and wriggled his way through the swing doors, the Colonel was nowhere to be seen.

'Um, most awkward,' muttered the Professor, 'I wonder which way he went. There seem to be an exceedingly large number of places here one might go.'

Just then a young lady carrying quantities of cushions went past, scraping most of the cushions off on the Professor, who ploughed his way through them, and ran smack into a man with an enormous arm-chair on his head.

'Dear, dear, what a most complicated business this furniture store sort of thing is to be sure,' spluttered the Professor, getting away from everyone, taking the first on the left and the second on the right, and finding himself tangled up in a forest of rolls of linoleum. 'Now I suppose Dedshott has got himself hidden in one of these things.' He started tipping the rolls over, but the Colonel didn't come out. Instead, a tall man with whiskers came up and said, 'If there is anything you are requiring, sir, will you allow me to show it to you.'

'I want Colonel Dedshott,' said the Professor. The long, thin man hustled the Professor into a lift, and they shot very slowly up to some other floors, while a resounding crash sounded below as someone dropped a tea-set.

'Now, sir,' he said, leading the Professor about

amongst welters of wardrobes, and corridors of cabinets, and terraces of tables, and stacks of sideboards, not to mention more chairs than could be sat on if everyone in Pagwell sat down at once, which they never did. 'I am sure you will like this one. It has folding doors and expanding legs. The top turns over and becomes an additional end, while, should you require more middle, you pull this lever, and the back portion becomes added to the front. A most remarkable sideboard, sir.'

'I don't want a sideboard, I want Colonel Dedshott,' cried the Professor, getting so tangled up he didn't even notice it was a sideboard of his own invention the thin man was trying to sell him. He hurried through a doorway, down a long corridor with lots of doors, at all of which he knocked, hoping to find Colonel Dedshott behind one of them. Out of one door came the girl with the cushions, carrying twice as many as before, accompanied by another girl with an enormous lampshade on her head and ten boxes in each hand. Out of another door came an advertising sort of man, with a long nose and a handful of papers ; while the last door hid a room so stacked up with little tables that as soon as the Professor opened the door hundreds of them poured out on him.

In the meantime, Colonel Dedshott was also looking for the Professor. He heard the crash of the tea-set, guessed it must be the Professor, but guessed wrong, and arrived in the china department just in time to be sold a pink china eggcup he didn't want.

'Branestawm! Branestawm!' roared the Colonel, who believed in shouting rather than searching.

A man came by with a lawn mower and four deckchairs, and nearly mowed the Colonel's trousers off.

A very jolly gentleman in the linen department was unfolding serviettes by the dozen, and making some less jolly-looking gentlemen fold them up again, so as to look busy.

'Branestawm, where are you?' thundered the Colonel. He ramped across the shop, followed closely by several electric standard lamps, because he'd caught his foot in their wires. Five old ladies were sitting in a row in front of a mountain of carpets, which two men, with dark faces and light overalls, were turning over one at a time. The Colonel watched, thinking the Professor might very likely be buried underneath. At last they got to the bottom of the carpets. The old ladies stood up, and filed slowly out of the shop without a word, while the head carpet man went away to see why someone had sent him a rug with the sides in the middle, and no edges at all.

'Will you show me some bookcases?' said a lady, and the Colonel, who was always a one for being gallant to the ladies, untangled himself from the electric lamps and led the way to where he hoped bookcases might be, but which turned out to be where nothing but aluminium frying-pans were.

'I –' began the Colonel, then suddenly down some stairs came Professor Branestawm, with little tables sticking out all over him, so they left it to someone else to explain to the lady the difference between frying-pans and bookcases, while they hurried through a department full of all the clocks in Pagwell, each showing a different time, past a counter with railings on it, and people on both sides paying money to each other with gleeful cries of 'one and nine, two shillings, four pounds two and tuppence, ten, nine, eight, four and a half's three and ninepence, correct, have you got two shillings for a sixpence, and change please, seven and a quarter two, eighteen shillings and elemfree.'

At last they arrived at a huge door, all studded with brass knobs, fitted with bells, and covered with labels saying 'In conference', and 'Not to be disturbed', and 'Private', and 'Beware of the Dog', and 'Rose Cottage', and 'Bathroom', some of which had got nailed on by mistake, and were really for sale.

Taking no notice of anything, the Colonel rapped on the door, hurting his knuckles and making no noticeable sound, opened the door and walked in.

'Ha, morning, Mr Chintsbitz,' he cried. 'Here is Professor Branestawm, who has a wonderful invention to show you. Jolly clever and all that, what!'

Mr Chintsbitz was a positively enormous man, with a big black beard. He was smoking a huge cigar so fiercely that it seemed more like a firework, and he always kept his hat on so that people in the shop shouldn't think he was anything to do with it, and go asking him to direct them to linoleums, or show them some supper cloths. He burst out of his chair, and shook hands with them so violently, that three of the Colonel's medals flew out of the window, and the Professor's five pairs of glasses flew all over the room.

'S'fine, siddown,' he boomed, running strings of words into one enormous word, 'Gladtoseeyou. Show me invention. Whassitallabout?' He sat down, and tilted his chair back on two legs, but tilted it a bit too far and it fell over with no end of a bang, landing Mr Chintsbitz in the none too large wastepaper basket, from which the Colonel and the Professor had all they could do and a bit over to get him out. Then the Professor found he'd forgotten what he'd come for, after

all the rushing about the shop, and nearly being sold sideboards.

'Invisible glass,' whispered the Colonel very hissily, not wanting Mr Chintsbitz to hear until they were ready to spring the invention on him a bit surprisingly.

'Oh, ah – er – um, yes, of course, of course,' mumbled the Professor. He fumbled in his pockets, and drew out fourpence in halfpennies, three old envelopes, one full of little cogwheels, several yards of assorted string, mostly with knots in, a stub of pencil with teeth-marks all over it, half a bun he'd forgotten to eat for his day before yesterday's tea, and finally a piece of the wonderful new non-shine glass.

'Er – there you are, what do you think of that?' he said proudly, holding the invisible glass out in front of Mr Chintsbitz's eyes.

Mr Chintsbitz blinked, and blew out torrents of smoke and sparks from his cigar. Of course he couldn't see any glass. It was invisible.

'Verrifunny,' he grunted, 'buttI'mabuzziman. Izzitajokeaniffsowhy?'

'Invisible glass,' said the Professor, tapping the glass with his fingers. 'Ordinary glass shines where it reflects the light. This glass does not reflect light, so you cannot see it. Now in the case of shop windows, as you know, the light and particularly the sunshine is often reflected from the glass into the eyes of people who are looking into the window, so that they are unable to see what is in the window that they are looking at without seeing it. That is to say –'

But Mr Chintsbitz didn't wait. He was quick at understanding things. He leapt to his feet, and hurled his cigar out of the window so drastically that it stuck firmly to the wall opposite, and went on smoking itself.

'Professor Branestawm,' he thundered, 'swonderful idea. Solvesabigproblemforus. Followme.' He swirled out of the room with the Colonel and the Professor doing their best to keep up. Through the shop he went like ten whirlwinds, and everybody immediately started being terrifically busy, doing anything or nothing, according to how quick they were at thinking of something. In fact, Mr Chintsbitz made everyone so nervous that several customers started doing jobs of work about the place, feeling he might get cross with them for standing about doing nothing. He shot through some turnstile sort of doors that spun round rapidly as he went through them, and the Colonel and the Professor, following behind, got themselves caught in the doors, and had to go round ten times before they could stop.

'Thereyouare,' boomed Mr Chintsbitz, waving his hand at one of the shop windows, which looked more like a looking-glass than a window, because the sun shone on it and reflected all the shops on the other side of the road. 'Can'tseeathing. Triedeverything. Allnogood. WhattaboutyourglassProfessor?'

Professor Branestawm immediately came over all technical. He talked about reflected light, and spectrums, and inclined planes, and transparent surfaces. He waved his hands about. He put on one pair of spectacles after another, and then several at once. Colonel Dedshott's head went round faster than it had ever gone before, which may have been due to the Colonel having gone round a bit fast in the revolving doors. Mr Chintsbitz listened with his eyes sticking out, and uttered a bunch of words in a lump now and then. At last it was agreed that the Professor should put his invisible non-shine glass into that one window, and see how it looked. Then they went across the road and had a cup of something each, except Mr Chintsbitz, who had four cups of everything.

Professor Branestawm rubbed his hands together, said 'Um, most excellent, better than I expected,' and put on most of his pairs of spectacles upside down in his excitement. Colonel Dedshott clicked his heels, jingled his medals, and said, 'My word, you know. Jolly clever, what!' while Mr Chintsbitz ran his hand through his enormous beard, 'SwonderfulI'mgladdi-metyou.'

They were standing in front of the window in the Pagwell Furnishing Company's shop which had been fitted with the Professor's non-shine glass. And the result was amazing. It looked as if there was no glass there. You could see everything in the window wonderfully clearly. You could even see the top of a window-dresser sort of man's head, which wasn't meant to be seen as he was behind somewhere, fixing something up with drawing-pins.

Mr Chintsbitz was so delighted he gave the Professor an order written on pink paper and signed in nine places to fit all the windows in the shop with the new glass.

For days and weeks Professor Branestawm was busy in his magnificent new Inventory, which he'd paid for with some of the treasure they'd found in the Did-dituptite Islands. He had no end of men in to help, and Mrs Flittersnoop was kept so busy bringing them cups of tea, and telling them to wipe their feet on the mat, that she had to have her sister Aggie, from Lower Pagwell, up to stay with her and give her a hand. It was a nice change from going down to stay with her sister, which she often did when the Professor's inventions went a bit bustable.

At last the work was finished. The sheets of invisible glass were carried out to a special sort of cart, and driven carefully round to the Pagwell Furnishing Store, where they were put into the windows instead of the old shiny glass. It was the very goodness-knows-what of a job, because sometimes the men couldn't find the piece of invisible glass they were using, sometimes they thought they'd done a window, when really they'd only taken the old glass out, and sometimes they tried to do the same window twice, and only found out it was done when they bumped their noses against the invisible glass.

But, after plenty of talking, and rather much arguing, and heaps of shouting, 'a bit more to you, Sam,' and 'ease her over here, Jim,' and 'give a hand with this, Harry,' and 'easy does it, boys,' and other workman kind of talk, the job was finished, and Professor Branestawm, who had been dancing round, getting in everybody's way a bit, and in his own way a tremendous amount, went home and had a basinful of sago pudding with cherries on it, which was an invention of Mrs Flittersnoop's.

Next day a frantic telegram came from the Pagwell Furnishing Company:

'Come-at-once-awful-disaster-your-attention-needed-at-once-good-gracious-hurry.'

All written as one enormous word, which was all right for Mr Chintsbitz, because with telegraphs at a penny a word it worked out nice and cheaply, but which was severely awkward for the telegram people, who had to turn it all into little dots and dashes and clicky noises, and then turn it back into letters, and a positive puzzle for the Professor, who started reading it from the wrong end, thinking it was a new sort of language, but not seeing how it could be.

As soon as he'd made it out, round to the Pagwell Furnishing Company he dashed. Everything was in several uproars. The glass in the windows was so invisible that lots of people had walked smack through it, thinking it wasn't there, and smashed it to invisible smithereens. And the wind was blowing in at some windows, and out at others, causing the most uncalled-for muddle in the shop. Some of the carpet men had got tangled up in the furniture department, and were trying to sell sideboards by the yard. A linen department man was doing his best to roll up a tea-set. Two ladies from the china part were wondering if six rugs and a carpet went to a set, like six tumblers and a jug. A gentleman who looked after curtains was doing his best to cut off a few yards of linoleum with little weeny scissors, but not getting very far, and the girl with the cushions had collapsed on a heap of them, and wasn't bothering to get up.

'My-goodness-look-at-this,' Mr Chintsbitz was roaring, ramping round in circles. 'Place-is-in-bits. Confound-your-glass. Do-something-about-it-never-mind-what.'

'I – er – um – ah, I never thought of this, to be sure,' moaned the Professor, looking round wildly at the fantastic and fuddled up furnishing that was going on all round him. 'I must make the glass thicker and stronger. Yes, yes, that is the only thing to do. These windows are so large, the glass breaks too easily. Dear me, I had no idea shops were such extremely difficult places to understand.'

Off he shot to his Inventory again, and got all his assistant men together, helping him to make more and thicker and stronger invisible glass. Mrs Flittersnoop's sister, Aggie, luckily hadn't gone home yet, which helped a bit, but not much. Boards had to be put up all over the Pagwell Furnishing Company's windows, and placards were put on them, saying 'Business as usual during alterations,' and 'Buy now,' and 'Smashing reductions,' which wasn't meant to refer to the windows, but people probably thought it was.

At last the new and thicker glass was made, and

got into the windows. The sideboards were got away from the carpets. The curtain gentleman was got away from the linoleum, which he came away from rather willingly. The tea-sets and rugs were sorted out, the cushion girl was stood right way up, and Mr Chintsbitz went out to have his hair cut, but came back looking very little different, as he refused to take off his hat while it was done.

'Well – er – thank goodness everything is all right now,' muttered the Professor. But, oh help and everything. Oh dearie, dearie. The very next morning ten telegrams arrived, with one word on each, saying several different things, according to which way you arranged them, but as the word 'catastrophe' occurred on two of them the Professor dashed frantically back to the Pagwell Furnishing Company.

What a sight met his gaze! What undreamed-of-happenings had occurred! Oh, oh, oh! Crowds of people thronged the streets. Everywhere was in a muddle. Even the one-way traffic was going both ways, but not going far because so many people were in the way.

Professor Branestawm's glass hadn't got broken this time. It was coming out in large bubbles all over itself. Yes, yes, it was. And the bubbles were rising up and bursting with a series of different-sounding pops, and cracks, and pings. And wherever a bubble came up, it shone like anything, and could be seen, but the rest of the glass remained invisible. It looked like an unseen giant, blowing bubbles from a non-existing pipe. No wonder there was a crowd. Pagwell had seen nothing like it.

Professor Branestawm's head began to go round just like Colonel Dedshott's always did when he described things to him. How could this incredible thing have happened? Had he forgotten to put any thingummy in the glass? Had he boiled it too long, or not baked it long enough? Had he got it mixed up with Mrs Flittersnoop's recipe for gooseberry jam, or what?

In the middle of his thoughts, Mr Chintsbitz came bursting through the crowd, with his beard waving about in the wind.

The Professor was just wondering whether it would be as well to run away and hide somewhere for a while, when Mr Chintsbitz's huge hand descended on his shoulder, and his enormous voice boomed in his ears.

'Dunno-how-it-happened-but-marvellous-thing,' he shouted. 'Best-attraction-we've-had-since-place-opened. Look-at-the-crowds.'

'I – er – that is –' spluttered the Professor, but Mr Chintsbitz swept him inside the shop, which was nearly as full of people as the streets outside. Tea-sets were being sold right and left. Carpets were being bought in layers. They were nearly sold out of sideboards. Seventeen people were all arguing as to who was to have the only bedroom suite that was left, a yellow one with green knobs. A gentleman, whose face was all smile and eye-glasses, had sold fifteen assorted armchairs that had been in stock for years. People were measuring off curtain material and roller towelling so fast that their hands nearly flew off the ends of their arms. The cushion girl had no cushions left to stagger about with, and was giving a hand with the clocks and lawn mowers, while at the place where the money was paid over, the air was thick with banknotes and coins, and cries of 'eightynine pounds, a hundred, twopence change, thank you.'

It was all astounding and wonderful. And it was all exceedingly pleasant for the Pagwell Furnishing Company. The Professor's bubbly glass had attracted everyone for miles around. People who had never been inside the shop came to see the unlikely glass, and also saw no end of things they felt they would like to have. Things were not only all right, but most deliriously, marvellously better than they had ever been.

Mr Chintsbitz dragged the Professor into his office, and collapsed with a crash into his chair.

'How-can-we-thank-you-Professor,' he burst out. 'This-has-made-business-wonderful.'

'B – but the glass may go on bubbling like that for ages,' stammered the Professor.

'All-the-better-if-it-does,' roared Mr Chintsbitz. 'Longer-it-goes-on-better-for-us. Look-at-the-crowds. When - it - stops - if - worst - comes - to - worst - can-put-back-ordinary-glass.'

He shook hands with the Professor until he nearly shook him to bits. Then they went out, and had the most astounding dinner together, with ten different kinds of vegetables, and enough lemonade to sink a ship. And most wonderful of all, Mr Chintsbitz took his hat off, probably for the first time in his life.

So all was well that ended none too badly, and, taking things all round, a good time was had by all.

3

Branestawm's Theatre

I⊤ was a great day for Mrs Flittersnoop when the Professor took her to the theatre.

As a rule Professor Branestawm never went to theatres, unless they were lecture theatres, and he had no interest in any stages but the stages of scientific experiments. But as someone had sent him a couple of tickets he thought he and Mrs Flittersnoop might sort of step out and hit the high spots for once.

So off they set half an hour too early, because Mrs Flittersnoop liked to be in plenty of time, in a taxi driven by Mrs Flittersnoop's sister Aggie's cousin Alfred, with Mrs Flittersnoop wearing Aggie's best feather boa she had kindly lent her, and the Professor so fastened up inside a very hard shirt, and a very tall collar, that he could barely manage to manipulate his five pairs of spectacles.

'Well, I must say this is a treat for me, sir, thanking you kindly,' said Mrs Flittersnoop, as they rattled along with the tuppences ticking up at every corner. 'Not that I don't enjoy a good play, as you might say, sir, though I can't say I'm one to hold with so much gallivanting as one sees the young people doing nowadays, sir.'

'Yes, yes, of course, – er – certainly,' said the Professor, who was a bit bothered through wanting to work out a new invention and having nothing to draw diagrams on except his nice stiff white shirt front, which he'd have drawn them on like a shot, only Mrs Flittersnoop had emptied his pockets before they came out, to make him look less bulgy, and he had nothing to draw with.

Presently they arrived at the theatre, and in due course Mrs Flittersnoop arrived in the right seat. But from the moment of stepping out of the taxi into a slight puddle she lost sight of Professor Branestawm, and didn't find him again until she found him waiting for his breakfast with diagrams all over the tablecloth next morning.

Of course, Professor Branestawm was always rather one for getting things wrong way round. So perhaps it isn't so very surprising that he went in at the stage-door by mistake and found himself among acres of scenery, forests of ropes and terrific quantities of drastically exaggerated lights, back stage of Pagwell Theatre Royal, instead of among the polite programme rustlers in the stalls.

'Um – ah, most instructive,' said the Professor, gazing around in delight. 'I had no idea theatres were like this. We must go more often, Mrs Flittersnoop.'

'Yes, I'm sure I should like to,' said Mrs Flittersnoop. But she said it sitting in the stalls to a girl in a teeny lace apron, who asked her if she'd like to have opera-glasses.

The Professor climbed cautiously up an exceedingly vertical ladder, trod on a rung that had been missing for a week, grabbed at the nearest rope to save himself from falling, and brought a painted forest down about his ears.

'Dear me, most extraordinary,' he gasped, staggering back against a lever that changed the painted forest

for a still more painted drawing-room. 'Most interesting, most um – ah – exciting.'

'Most exciting, I'm sure,' agreed Mrs Flittersnoop in the stalls as the orchestra began to tune up.

Then scene-shifting sorts of men descended on the Professor from all directions. He got away from them and hid behind an imitation mountain, making frantic and greasy notes on his shirt front with an eyebrow pencil one of the actress ladies had dropped ; while Mrs Flittersnoop applauded loudly. But that was for the play, which she was enjoying, probably none the less for the Professor's absence.

Professor Branestawm's theatre, of course, was bound to happen after that.

'The important thing to my mind in theatre design,' he said to Colonel Dedshott, 'is to arrange matters so that the – er – scenery may be changed – ah – rapidly. No waits, Dedshott. No waits.'

'Ha, yes, by jove, rather not!' said the Colonel, who didn't agree with waiting for anything more than three-quarters of a second.

The Professor's first idea for a rapid scene-changing theatre was to have ten stages in a semicircular row and use them one at a time.

'Each time a fresh stage comes into use,' he explained, 'the part where the spectators sit automatically moves round to face it.'

'How about exits in case of fire?' asked a Pagwell councillor, who had come to see what he could prohibit.

'Entrance and exit would be made through the roof,' said the Professor. 'But I have since discarded that theory for another – ah – better one.'

The second idea was to have each spectator's seat turn round on its own sort of spindle to face the different stages as they came into use.

'But, dear me,' said the Vicar of Pagwell, who was interested in theatres, as he organized charades in aid of things at Christmas. 'Surely that will mean that people who have paid for the best front seats will eventually find themselves at the back.'

That squashed idea number two.

The third plan was really terrific.

Professor Branestawm was going to have a tower, with six stages, one above the other, all ready set with different scenes, and lower it bit by bit to bring the various scenes into position behind the proscenium in turn.

'There could be music to hide the sound of the stages moving down,' said the Professor.

But as that would have meant not only a tower even higher than the spire of Pagwell Church, but also a sort of young mineshaft going down the same distance into the earth, idea number three was finally sat on by his friend before the Professor could start anything dangerous with it.

At last the final plans for the theatre were completed, and they included, not one of the Professor's ideas but positively several. They also included a good bundle of notions the Professor had got from Pagwell Theatre, West Pagwell Steam Laundry, some toys belonging to Mrs Flittersnoop's sister Aggie's nephew, and a book on marionettes from Pagwell Gardens Library.

Excitable activity began to take place in Pagwell. Tall sorts of knitted metal cranes rose up like industrial maypoles with chains hanging all over the place.

Rows upon rows of gentlemen with their garters outside their trousers dug down so far they disappeared from sight. Mechanical sorts of gentlemen in fetching blue overalls clanged away among gigantic cogwheels. And in, out, round about strode Professor Branestawm, with his five pairs of spectacles fastened on with string owing to windy weather, accompanied by surveyor sorts of gentlemen carrying twisted telescopes and striped walking-sticks, architect sorts of gentlemen bulging with rolls of plans and mechanical ready-reckoners, and Mrs Flittersnoop's sister Aggie's little girl carrying the Professor's lunch done up in a red handkerchief, which was an idea the Professor had got from the digging gentlemen.

There was a small spot of bother at first over getting ready the first play for the Professor's theatre.

The Professor's idea of a suitable play was one in which frequent and tremendous changes of scenery could take place, where there was lots of scope for terrific transformations, luxurious lighting and no end of mechanical miracles.

The actors' idea was to do a great deal of foot stamping and hand waving, shake with passion, laugh with joy, burst into tears and shrink with horror as often as possible in assorted attitudes.

The author's idea was to have everyone saying as much as possible in different kinds of high-class language.

The difficulty was sort of solved by the actors agreeing with the Professor while he was there and putting back all the things he had altered when he went away to study the machinery, which he did very often.

The first night of the first play at Branestawm's theatre was an event surpassing anything that had happened in Pagwell since the Professor nearly blew up the gasworks with an insufficiently tamed invention.

Everyone of importance was there as tickets had been given away with the Professor's compliments. The Mayor and a careful selection of Pagwell councillors were in the boxes. The Vicar was with his twin daughters, Maisie and Daisie, both dressed alike and both eating the same sort of chocolates. Doctor Mumpzanmeazle hoped to pop in and see some of the play if people would leave off being ill long enough to let him. The Pagwell tradesmen sat in clean collars and blue suits in well behaved rows in the circle, and Mrs Flittersnoop, accompanied by sister Aggie and taking it in turns to wear sister Aggie's feather boa, had three seats to the two of them, so that they could change places when they felt like it.

Behind the scenes the Professor, wearing a false moustache to help him feel at home, was running round giving last-minute instructions to the actors and final drops of oil to the scene-changing machinery.

The orchestra struck up. The lights dimmed down. Chocolate eating was subdued and the curtain rose all the way up first go without sticking anywhere.

'Bravo, Branestawm. Stuff to give 'em – by jove, what!' grunted Colonel Dedshott, who was standing at the back with a detachment of Catapult Cavaliers in case of trouble.

Everything started very well. The actors stamped and waved and were sad, joyous or frightened in the right places. Scenes changed as if by magic as the Professor pulled levers and twiddled wheels. Nobody threw anything except an actress lady who threw a jug.

'Very good, I'm sure, sir,' said Mrs Flittersnoop.

'Really a most creditable performance, my dear Professor,' murmured the Vicar.

'Whoopee,' agreed Maisie and Daisie.

Then complications began to set in.

The actors were saying all the words and singing all the songs the Professor had reckoned on not having done. The Professor was so delighted at the unexpected workability of his theatrical engines that he changed the scenery as fast as he could go. Used it all up before the play was halfway through and had to start over again. The actors hurried and hustled through their acting to try to catch up with the scenery. The audience dared not applaud in case they missed a scene or two.

Then the Professor's false moustache fell off into the works. Theatrical machinery is evidently very touchy. Professor Branestawm's was anyway. In half a song and two-sevenths of a scene it had got the better of the Professor.

'Um, dear me, I feel this will be a little awkward,' he muttered, as half a forest and two-thirds of a heavy bedroom descended upon a polite drawing-room tea party scene.

As the first part of this was the cue for the chorus to dance on from all sides, dressed as elves, on they had to dance. But the scene had gone off so much too soon that most of them were only half dressed. But nobody in the theatre noticed that, except the Vicar, who thought that something should be done about it, only couldn't think what.

Behind the scenes the Professor was also thinking something must be done about things, and he could think what. It was rather a pity he could really. He pulled over a handful of levers and the forest-cum-

bedroom scene was whirled away to reveal a rocky cavern full of office furniture and elephants.

'Tut, tut, this is really most annoying,' he muttered.

He pulled a rope. Down came a considerable helping of fifteenth-century castle and scooped the Professor up into a corner while the scene-changing machinery went merrily on by itself.

The castle scene became in rapid succession a view of the sea coast with an oak ceiling and Chinese pagodas. A street in Spain containing the entrance to Kew Gardens. A kitchen scene with tropical trees growing inside it, and a dockyard setting upside down with sideways flower borders and some back-to-front portions of modern dining-room.

'My word, by jove, what!' gasped Colonel Dedshott, guessing something had gone wrong.

A vital duet between a terrific tenor and a solid soprano was cut short by an uncalled-for thunderstorm accompanied by train noises. There was a shipwreck inside an Oriental palace. Another singing gentleman coming on for a song was swallowed up by a trap-door before he could sing a note of it, and the orchestra went up on stalks and got mixed up with the flying ballet who were wearing blue bowler hats, partly because of hurried changing and partly owing to disobedient lighting effects.

The Professor got out from behind the castle scenery and rushed to his levers.

'Must stop it at all costs,' he cried. 'Dear, dear, most disturbing.'

Three drawing-room scenes with assorted ceilings.

'Very good, I'm sure,' said Mrs Flittersnoop in the stalls.

'Surely this is contrary to the bye-laws,' said the

Mayor, up in a box, as a piece of stage came up and blew cardboard snow all over him.

Forests and factories. Streets and staircases. 'Dear me, most awkward.' Fairies in trousers. Coloured clouds underfoot. 'By jove, sir, what!' Crash. Ta – ar a – zim – tiddlyom 'Oo-er, choc-lits!'

The Professor tripped over a discarded actor and fell on the machinery. All the scenery in stock came down at once. The orchestra collapsed in a musical heap, then the curtain came right down and fell in folds over the footlights.

'I fear, Dedshott, that my excursions into the realms of theatrical art have not been altogether – ah – successful,' said the Professor next day.

But that's where he was wrong.

The audience had thought everything had been done on purpose, for fun, and had laughed so much some of them had to stay the night at the theatre as they felt too weak to go home. And the show ran for three thousand performances, all different, with special people behind the scenes ready to cut a rope or throw a brick into the works if things threatened to go right instead of wrong.

4

The Disappearing Abolisher

COLONEL DEDSHOTT of the Catapult Cavaliers knocked heartily on the Professor's front door at exactly the same moment that Mrs Flittersnoop, the Professor's housekeeper, was knocking politely on his study door.

The Professor happened to look through the window and saw the Colonel on the step.

'Ah – er – um, my dear Dedshott, come in, come in,' he said, making for the door.

Mrs Flittersnoop heard him say 'come in,' and she came in, tea tray and all, just as the Professor came out. The result was a most resounding teatime crash. Showers of brown bread and butter, hailstones of Bath buns, and plenty of steam.

Colonel Dedshott thought the Professor was having trouble with burglars or something and climbed hastily through the window, where he got tangled up with the Professor's latest invention, and had to be unravelled like so much unsuccessful knitting.

'Well, Branestawm, what's the invention this time?' said the Colonel, when they were settled with more tea, fresh bread and butter, and the same Bath buns, carefully dusted and re-arranged. 'Talking pictures, what? Or a new kind of machine for adding up one's pocket-money, ha ha!'

The Professor looked at him through a special pair of spectacles with little lids on them.

'An idea of far-reaching – er – importance, Ded-shott,' he said, reaching a bit far himself for another bun. 'Branestawm's Disappearing Abolisher.'

'Wonderful,' said the Colonel.

'If this lens,' explained the Professor, pointing to a sticking-out part of the machine, like a sort of sideways chimney, 'is directed towards any person or object within a given distance and this red button is pressed, the said object or person instantly – um, ah – disappears,' finished the Professor.

'But,' he went on, 'that is not all. You see these other buttons, Dedshott, the white one is the reappearing button. Press it and your disappeared object re – ah – appears.' He shut down the lids of his spectacles and wheeled the invention forward. 'The other button, Dedshott,' he said excitedly, 'the black one, is the abolishing button.'

'Marvellous,' said the Colonel. 'Don't know how you think of these things, by jove.'

'There are two ways in which the object or – er – person may be caused to vanish,' continued the Professor. 'They may be simply – er – disappeared. That is to say, they become invisible. They cannot be seen. But they are still there, Dedshott.'

'Ha, yes, of course,' agreed the Colonel.

'The second method,' went on the Professor, waving spectacles and bread and butter about, 'I call abolishing. Having disappeared something or someone by pressing the red button, I have only to press the black button and they become abolished entirely. They are not only invisible, Dedshott. They are not there at all.'

The Colonel said nothing. His head was going round and round, and he was content not to listen much, and agree with everything.

'When I have disappeared an object I can reappear it by pressing this white button,' went on the Professor. 'But the thing once abolished with the black button is gone for ever. I will show you.'

The Professor focused his machine on the teapot and pressed the red button.

'Squee-e-e pop.' There was a faint blue haze and the teapot vanished, but the tea made in it did not, which made a somewhat mess on the traycloth.

'I press the white button,' said the Professor, 'and, *voilà*.' *Voilà* it was.

Back came the teapot with more blue haze and pops.

'Bravo! My word, Branestawm, jolly clever, what!' cried the Colonel.

'I have not – er – finished, Dedshott,' said the Professor. He aimed his machine at a pink vase. Pressed the red button. Squee-e-e pop. Blue haze, no pink vase. Also not so many whiskers on the Colonel's moustache, as he had got himself a bit in the way of the disappearing demonstration.

'Bravo!' said the Colonel, who never cared much for pink vases, and didn't know about his whiskers.

'The vase has disappeared, but it is still there,' said the Professor. 'Just – er – pass your hands along the mantelpiece, Dedshott, and satisfy yourself on that point.'

The Colonel felt about and found there was a hard, vase-shaped something where the pink ornament had been.

'I now press the black abolishing button,' said the Professor.

He pressed it. There was a small bang and two puffs of smoke, one green and one dirty.

'Now see if you can find the vase,' he chuckled.

The Colonel tried. There was no vase-shaped something.

'Completely abolished,' said the Professor. 'Nothing can bring that vase back again.'

'Um – ha,' grunted the Colonel.

'I am demonstrating the machine at Pagwell College next Tuesday,' said the Professor. 'Mr Stinckz-Bernagh, the science master, persuaded me to agree, but I – ah – fear I have very little experience of lecturing to boys. I wonder if you would – ah – um – care to come with me, Dedshott, by way of maintaining discipline.'

Anything to do with discipline was the Colonel's middle name. Certainly he would be there. In full-dress uniform, wearing his medals and his best pair of spurs. The Professor could count on him. Discipline. If the demonstration depended on that it was an assured success, his word, by jove, yes, sir!

Getting the Professor's invention delivered to Pagwell College was a definitely touchy business. The manager of the Pagwell Furnishing Stores had kindly lent his biggest van and quantities of heavy gentlemen in aprons. The Professor insisted on riding inside the van with the invention to hold it together going round corners, as the van looked like being definitely shakable.

Once, when the van stopped suddenly at some traffic lights, the Professor sat on the machine and disappeared the van. He got it visible again only just in time to prevent three buses and a coal cart from running into it.

At Pagwell College most of the doors were too narrow to get the invention through. The moving-men, to whom the Professor had been doing a bit of complicated explaining on the way, were all for abolishing a bit of wall and unabolishing it after they had got the machine through, not seeing why an abolished thing had to stay abolished if a disappeared one could be visibled again.

At last the problem solved itself by two-thirds of the invention coming off in the Professor's hands during the pushing about process. So it went in comfortably, and the Professor had it all fastened together again in the wrong classroom before anyone could stop him. This meant that the sixth form, all rather long-shaped boys in almost grown-up trousers, had to wedge themselves into little pale-blue desks in a room with joyous animals all over the walls. For the Professor had set his machine up in the Kindergarten.

Presently the door opened and in swept Mr Stinckz-Bernagh in a schoolmaster's gown, so flowing, and so much torn into strips at the edges, that he looked like a rapid black comet with too many tails.

'Good morning, Professor, we are honoured by your presence and looking forward to your demonstration which, I am sure, will be of the utmost educational value,' he said in a very thin, crisp voice. Then he gathered up all the ends of his gown in both hands, dumped them on a table, leant on the top of them, and glared at the sixth-formers, who were sitting motionless, looking even more innocent and cherubic than the five-year-olds who usually sat in that room.

'Professor Branestawm has come here at great trouble and expense to lecture you on his own invention, which is exceedingly good of him. Three cheers for the Professor. Hurray! Hurray! Hurray!' said Mr Stinckz-Bernagh, who believed in doing all the polite things,

but didn't believe in wasting any time in doing them. 'May I remind you,' he went on, 'that there is a football match on Saturday afternoon in which I believe most of you hope to play. I trust it will not be necessary to postpone the match owing to some of you being kept in as a result of your not behaving properly during the Professor's lecture.'

Then he gave out fifty lines all round to start with, and said that those who attended properly would not be expected to do them, swooshed his gown off the table, said, 'Kindly begin, Professor,' and disappeared out of the door in a shower of white chalk, dust, and black ribbons.

Professor Branestawm arranged his five pairs of spectacles in lecturing attitudes and began, while Colonel Dedshott stood by the door, military and menacing, ready to quell the slightest sign of revolt.

'Please, sir, may I go and get a handkerchief?' asked a boy with red hair and freckles, sticking up his hand.

'Er – um – ah, yes, of course,' said the Professor, stopping in the middle of a complicated piece of explanatory finger-twiddling.

'Can I get one too, sir?' chirped a boy with a long nose that had ink smudges on it.

'I've left mine in my overcoat too,' said another. 'Me too,' said several more.

The first ten minutes of the lecture passed to the tune of tramping feet as the class charged in and out for handkerchiefs. The Professor clashed his spectacles and felt as bewildered as his explanation of inventions usually made other people.

Colonel Dedshott, determined to have discipline at all costs, grunted 'left, right, left, right, pick up your feet, now,' as the scholars marched in and out on the handkerchief parade.

'Now this lens –' began the Professor again when everyone had all the handkerchiefs they could do with.

Red-head-and-freckles blew his nose like a trumpet.

'– when focused upon a given object,' said the Professor.

Nose-blowing broke out in a chorus up and down the class.

'Please may I go and get a pencil?' asked Red-head.

'Yes, yes!' muttered the Professor. 'Now this black button is most important, it is the abolishing –'

Crash! The Professor nearly jumped out of his spectacles. Had his machine accidentally abolished someone? No. Inky-nose had secretly tipped over the desk in front of him, boy and all.

By the time things had been put right way up and a second nose-blowing outbreak had passed, Colonel Dedshott noticed that Red-head hadn't come back from getting a pencil.

'Ha, deserter, what!' he grunted. 'Carry on, Brane-stawm, I'll fetch the defaulter. My word, yes,' and out he strode, while the Professor turned his invention round and began on the other side.

Presently a desk lid was gingerly raised and some careful rummaging about began. Another desk lid went up, then another, and another.

'Have the goodness to shut those – er – desks and attend to my – ah – lecture,' said the Professor, waving his near-sighted glasses threateningly.

Bang, bang, slam, crash! Desk lid-closing broke out like machine-gun fire.

Then the Professor began to notice something queer about the appearance of some of the scholars.

One was wearing a paper hat from one of the Kindergarten's drawing-books, so that it had some drawings of wobbly houses with wire smoke coming out of the chimneys chalked all over it.

'Stop that noise, by jove, what!' said the boy out of the side of his mouth in a Colonel Dedshott sort of voice.

Another pupil had made himself five enormous pairs of paper spectacles which he was wearing round his neck. Two others had their week's pocket-money fixed to their jackets with paper clips in imitation of Colonel Dedshott's medals.

The Professor made up his mind to take no notice of anything and get the lecture done as soon as possible. He charged on with complicated explanations, while the class gradually got more and more fantastic as paper hats and meant-to-be medals blossomed out in all directions.

'A peculiar mixture of light-rays is then directed upon the object,' went on the Professor.

'Can I go out and wipe my boots?' said Inky-nose.

'The black button is vitally important.' Three more paper hats and six rows of penny medals. 'Please, sir, he's taken my nibs.' 'Here you see a lever which controls the focusing adjustment.' Crash! 'Give me back my pencil.' 'Please, sir, can I go out and bring myself back?' Thump! 'Who put chalk in my ear?' 'Press the white button.'

In the midst of this educational uproar the door burst open and Colonel Dedshott returned triumphant, with Red-head grasped by one ear.

'By jove, what's this – mutiny!' said the Colonel. He advanced upon the class, every member of which was now completely equipped with paper hat, enormous spectacles, and pocket-money medals.

Then someone threw a ball of paper.

Pandemonium broke out.

The Colonel charged round knocking off paper hats with a ruler. Pocket-money clanged and tinkled over the floor. Red-head and Inky-nose barricaded themselves behind the blackboard and opened fire with bits of chalk.

Then the Professor lost his temper. He focused the disappearing abolisher on the rebels behind the blackboard and pressed the disappearing button. Bing! No Red-head. No Inky-nose.

But if the Professor thought that that was going to stop them he was mistaken. They had the advantage now. They were invisible, but still there. Unseen mischief occurred everywhere at once. Books flew through the air. Desks went crashing down. The Colonel's hat was snatched off and went dancing round the room, apparently on its own.

'Stop this at once, by jove, confound it, sir, what!'

roared the Colonel. He and the Professor tried to chase the invisible ringleaders into a corner. They dodged easily. Then Red-head had an idea. Yes, he did. He ran invisibly to the disappearing abolisher. He focused it on the Professor. He pressed the red button. Bing! Then, 'Oh help, no, no, don't do it, Red-head.' He pressed the awful black button. Zim!

Professor Branestawm himself was disastrously disappeared and unreturnably abolished by his own invention!

The door flew open and Mr Stinckz-Bernagh shot in.

The entire class sat motionless and innocent-looking. Not a paper hat or a penny medal was to be seen. Angelic expressions were on every face, even on the faces of Red-head and Inky-nose, who were invisible, but probably didn't know it.

Colonel Dedshott blew up.

'Disgraceful sir, by jove, someone shall hear of this, what! Is this how you maintain discipline in your school, confound it, sir? Professor Branestawm comes here to give a lecture and your boys behave like rebels, sir. Yes, by jove, mutiny, nothing less!'

'Where is the Professor?' asked Mr Stinckz-Bernagh in a calm and meant-to-be soothing voice he used for pacifying fearsome parents who sometimes complained if their little boys got themselves whacked.

The Colonel looked wildly round. Suddenly it dawned on him what had happened. Almost. He guessed the boys had disappeared the Professor, but not that they had abolished him too. With a roar he swept Mr Stinckz-Bernagh into the waste-paper basket and slammed down the white button on the machine with such force that the two disappeared boys, Red-head and Inky-nose, literally sprang into view with a couple of bangs.

But, of course, no Professor Branestawm came back with them. He was abolished. Oh dear, oh dear, what would Mrs Flittersnoop do? How would Pagwell Council manage when they wanted queer machines for doing unnecessary things? Colonel Dedshott's head would never go round and round again, listening to the Professor's explanations. They would never have uncalled-for tea parties together, getting bits of the invention mixed up with the food.

Colonel Dedshott couldn't stand the thought of it. Why hadn't he smashed the invention as he had smashed so many others before it could do any real harm? Dashing an unmilitary tear from his eye, he snatched up the easel, swung it up and was just about to bring it down on the disappearing abolisher when a hand restrained him.

It was Mr Stinckz-Bernagh, with the waste-paper basket still clinging to bits of his gown.

'Wait a moment,' he said. 'There is, I think, a better way. The Professor explained the working of his machine to me. If it can abolish its inventor, it can be made to abolish itself.'

He hurried out of the classroom and returned with a large mirror, which he set up opposite the machine.

'Ha!' grunted the Colonel.

'The light-rays focused on the mirror will be reflected back upon the machine,' began Mr Stinckz-Bernagh, starting to talk like the Professor himself.

Colonel Dedshott didn't wait for explanations. Viciously he slammed down all three buttons at once.

Crash, bang, whizz-z-z; pouff, wallop, zang, bump!

Pagwell College shook to its foundations. The air

was full of blue haze and pink dust. Colonel Dedshott and Mr Stinckz-Bernagh were flung simultaneously back into the waste-paper basket, which burst with another crash. The scholars tried to hide under the desks and got stuck there. Even the head master, who was at home with the tummy-ache, felt queer and shaky.

The disappearing abolisher had gone. Not so much as a lever or half a cog was left. The mirror was shattered to dust.

But, ah, oh, yes, but lovely and delightful and unexpected thing. In the place where the machine had been standing stood Professor Branestawm, clutching in one hand his five pairs of spectacles and in the other Mrs Flittersnoop's previously abolished pink vase.

'Er – um, dear me, most interesting and extraordinary,' muttered the Professor.

Colonel Dedshott rushed at him with open arms and Mr Stinckz-Bernagh only just got out of the way in time to avoid being tangled up in a mixture of medals and spectacles.

It may be a scientific fact that when a Disappearing Abolisher is itself abolished its previously abolished victims become unabolished. But it is also possible that the Professor's invention, while appearing all too successful, had in reality some little but vital thing wrong with it which prevented really permanent abolishing. Still, the machine itself was abolished all right. Thank goodness perhaps. And for once the Professor had no need to think of new ways of using up an invention. Instead he set out to write a book on 'What it feels like to be abolished,' but found he couldn't remember.

5

Branestawm's Eleven

A CRICKET ball zimmed through the window of Professor Branestawm's Inventory, which was, fortunately, open, so no glass got itself smashed.

'Please, can we have our ball back?' asked one of the cricket-playing little boys outside.

'Er – um – ah – hold this end of the wire while I fasten the other end,' said the Professor, giving him the wrong end of the right wire. Then he trod on the cricket ball and collapsed in a shower of not-yet-workable invention.

That got the Professor rather mixed up all round and, almost before he quite knew what was happening, he was playing cricket with the little boys, hitting the most accidentally mighty ones and bringing off exceedingly unintentional catches.

Then Colonel Dedshott arrived and fiercely shooed the boys away before he noticed the Professor. He wasn't very noticeable anyway, because he'd just seen what he thought might be a new kind of dandelion, but which was an ordinary kind of one with a toffee paper stuck on it.

'This – er – cricket sort of game, Dedshott, seems to – ah – suggest to me certain technical possibilities on the scientific side,' said the Professor.

'Ha ha, yes, rather!' said the Colonel, thinking he might as well be a bit jolly. 'Why don't you get up a team – what?'

'The – er – thought had occurred to me, Dedshott,' said the Professor.

'Hey?' said the Colonel in surprise.

'It would indeed be amusing,' he said, 'if I, Theophilus Branestawm, who have, I fear, been denied my share of fame in the more rarefied fields of intellectual activity, should become celebrated in an apparently frivolous field, such as that in which the game of cricket is – er – played.'

Before the Colonel had time to work out this rather complicated joke, the Professor had padded into his study and was looking up everything connected with cricket. He found that stumps are the bottom ends of trees that have been cut down. That bats are often found in belfries. That a wicket is a sort of small gate and that slips are sometimes worn while bathing.

Then Colonel Dedshott went home feeling as if his head was not only going round and round, but over and over as well, but not before the Professor had made him promise to arrange a sort of cricket committee meeting at the Vicar of Pagwell's next day.

Professor Branestawm's Cricket Inquiring Into Committee were on the Vicar's lawn in chairs just vacated by the ladies' sewing club. Except Colonel Dedshott, who had got rather hurriedly out of a chair that had been insufficiently vacated to the extent of three pins and a needle left sticking in the seat.

'I am sure we shall all be delighted to arrange a match for the Professor's team,' said the Vicar, 'and it gives me great pleasuah to permit the game to – ah – take place on the Vicarage field, providing the date does not clash with the children's picnic tea.'

'Anything in the nature of dangerous practices

would not be allowed by the bye-laws,' said the Mayor.

'Cricket's a slow old lark anyway,' put in Maisie and Daisie, the Vicar's twin daughters. 'If the Professor's got any cute ideas for pepping it up, I vote we let him try.'

'Well, let's get down to selecting a team,' said the Pagwell College Games Master, pulling out sheaves of paper with 'I must not eat sweets in school' written hundreds of times on one side.

By the time everyone whom everyone wanted to play had been put down there were twenty-seven players. But after a slight interval, during which the Vicar's wife handed round rather pale lemonade and some home-made cakes the sewing club hadn't been equal to, the team was got down to eleven men and one spare, although two of the men were ladies, Maisie and Daisie, who threatened to get up a dance and keep the rest of the team away on the day of the match if they weren't allowed to play.

The team consisted of:

Professor Branestawm, because it was his idea.

Colonel Dedshott, because he could be plentifully bashy when necessary.

The Vicar, because he was lending the field.

Mr Chintsbitz, Manager of the Pagwell Furnishing Stores, because he would lend a marquee for teas.

Dr Mumpzanmeazle, in case anyone got hit anywhere.

Maisie and Daisie, for reasons already stated.

Tom Wiglets
Hipdoodle's Bert } because they had stumps and
Wally Pyback } bats and things.

The Pagwell College Games Master, because he
   knew something about cricket.
And, as spare man, the Manager of Pagwell Penny
   Bank, because he could add up the score and probably get it right first time.

A match was then arranged with the Pagwell tradesmen for an early closing afternoon.

The Vicarage field, when arranged for Professor
Branestawm's cricket match, looked like a preparation
for elaborate obstacle races. There were two special
radio-active wickets which, as the Professor explained,

announced in a loud voice whether the batsman was out or not after each ball, thus making umpire kinds of people unnecessary. 'There are no – er – bails to – um – ah – adjust,' he pointed out, 'and the wickets are entirely self-acting.'

Nobody minded that as it didn't change any rules, but there were some energetic arguments about the Professor's clockwork bowling machine with its speed regulator and buttons to push, according to whether you wanted googlies, yorkers, lobs, spins, or Pagwell twirlers. The last was a special kind invented by the Professor in which the ball went over the batsman's head and came back on the wicket from behind. It was eventually agreed that the machine could be used by both sides to make things fair, but the Pagwell twirlers were off.

Branestawm's eleven were to go in first, and the Professor, with his five pairs of spectacles tied on with string, partnered by Colonel Dedshott, opened the innings, while the Pagwell Tradesmen arranged themselves about the field in cricket-playing attitudes. The team included: Mr Draper, the Blacksmith; Mr Smith, the Florist; Mr Flower, the Ironmonger; Mr Ironmonger, the Baker; Mr Baker, the Butcher; Mr Butcher, the Carpenter; Mr Carpenter, the Garage man; Mr Carr, the Fishmonger; Mr Fish, the Jeweller; Mr Pearl, the Gardener, and Mr Gardiner, the Draper, which made it sound more like Happy Families than cricket, as far as the side was concerned.

Mr Baker, the Butcher, pressed the googlie button, but the ball went towards Colonel Dedshott because the Professor had stood himself at the wrong end.

'Ha,' grunted the Colonel, and walloped it clean over the fence on to a passing bus where it had five pennyworth of free ride and was finally taken home by an old lady for her doggie.

'Not out,' sang the wicket, and the Pagwell Penny Bank Manager put down a six.

Mr Baker touched the yorker button and another ball came hurtling towards the Colonel.

'That is another advantage of my bowling machine which I forgot to point out,' explained the Professor to Mr Baker. 'It delivers a new ball each time, and so avoids delays caused by looking for possibly lost ones.'

Meantime Colonel Dedshott had cut the yorker kind of ball very snickily between Mr Fish, the Jeweller, and Mr Ironmonger, the Baker, who collapsed in each other's arms trying to reach it, and the Colonel came thundering down the pitch to the Professor.

'Run, Branestawm, run!' he shouted.

'What did you say, Dedshott?' asked the Professor.

The Colonel puffed and spluttered, saw that Mr Flower, the Ironmonger, was about to slam the ball at his wicket, and darted back again, never mind if it counted as a run or not. But the Professor suddenly realized he was in a match and started running too, so they both got to the other wicket together, and the Colonel only just managed to dash back to the opposite end in time to avoid being run out.

That left Professor Branestawm to face the bowling and the Bank Manager to face the problem of how many runs it counted when the Professor did one and the Colonel three.

Mr Baker, the Butcher, thought he'd better keep friendly with the Professor as Mrs Flittersnoop had been complaining about the sausages lately. So he pressed another button and sent along a nice easy lobby sort of ball that anyone could have hit miles without knowing anything about cricket.

But the Professor had read no end of heavy books on batting and meant to start cautiously. He just held his bat so that the ball bonked into it and rolled aside a few inches.

'Bravo!' cried the Colonel encouragingly.

Mr Baker sent along another lobby one and the Professor felt so perky about not being out first ball that he took a mighty slam and missed the ball by yards, and fortunately it missed his wicket by inches. But he hit instead the ball that had been sort of left over from before, and made three runs and another headache for the Bank Manager.

Colonel Dedshott was in action again. He cut one past the Blacksmith for a straightforward two, and the one after that went clean through a hole in the marquee, where Mrs Flittersnoop, sister Aggie's little girl, and the Vicar's wife were getting tea and lemonade ready. Crash into an urn of the Professor's invention, which began pouring out cups of not-ready tea in the lemonade glasses.

'Over,' cried the bowling machine, and while the Bakers, and Drapers, and Fishmongers changed places, the machine put up a little flag, went 'toot, toot,' and chugged along to the other end of the pitch.

Then the game began to warm up. Colonel Dedshott knocked up forty-five, including three doubtful ones, which the Bank Manager put down on a separate little account he'd opened for rummy scores.

The Vicar made three gentle, single ones without hurting anyone, and came back smiling like Harvest Festival.

Doctor Mumpzanmeazle scored fifteen before a

whizzy yorker got him, middle stump, and made the wicket squeak 'out,' like someone who has been unexpectedly pinched.

The Pagwell College Games Master, who was practically the only one in a complete set of flannels, did some very ornamental work, made a pretty twenty-eight, and went back to talk to Maisie and Daisie while Tom Wiglets, Hipdoodle's Bert, and Wally Pyback sloshed away to the tune of seventeen between them.

Professor Branestawm seemed to bear a charmed life. He couldn't get out – possibly because the runs got scored in a way that only very occasionally left him to do any batting.

Mr Chintsbitz crashed off a brisk and bashy dozen or so, some of which were partly due to the ball getting lost in his whiskers and not dropping out until he'd run a few. Then at last the Professor was stumped. That left Maisie and Daisie to finish the innings, which they did by Maisie batting the first ball straight down into Daisie's wicket.

The first of the Tradesmen's team went in to bat to the accompaniment of slight cheers.

The plan of campaign seemed to consist of making as many runs as they jolly well could. And, in spite of some amazing catches which Colonel Dedshott brought off – mostly by accident – and in spite of the Professor varying the bowling so much that nobody, especially himself, knew what the ball was going to do next, the Tradesmen's team finished up with nearly twice as many runs as the Professor's side.

'Ha. Excellent game, what!' panted the Colonel, mopping his forehead with one hand and trying to hold a cup of tea and four different kinds of cake with the other. 'Good work, but we're not beaten yet, by jove,' he said to Mr Ironmonger, the Baker.

'Aye,' said Mr Ironmonger, munching two jam tarts placed open sides together in the baker's-shop fashion.

'It is quite a mistake to imagine,' the Professor was saying to the Vicar as he tried to drink a bun and break a piece off a cup of tea, 'that making a great number of runs is the entire – er – science of cricket.'

'My dear Professor, I quite agree with you,' said the Vicar, putting down his fifth cup on the saucer after putting the contents down inside himself. 'Of course, most decidedly, my dear sir. Dear me, what a poor look-out it would be for sport if it were so. Tut, tut, yes.'

The Professor, who was beginning to get used to the unscientific aspect of cricket, began the second innings, making the very dickens of a lot of runs, whether it was a mistake to imagine they were the whole science of cricket or not. Even the Colonel, at the other end, who was always at his best when fighting against fearful odds, and was slamming the bowling in all directions, was outshone by the Professor.

'Dear me,' he said, putting his spectacles straight after hitting a ball clank into the Vicarage dustbin for the third time in succession. 'I trust I am not – er – taking more than my – um – ha – share of this hitting business.'

Crack, smack, wallop, zim! 'Bravo, Branestawm.' Zizz, wallop! 'Boundary again! By jove, sir!' Bong! Vicarage dustbin again for four. 'Um, most satisfactory.' Crash through the tea marquee again, which didn't matter, as tea was over.

The Professor and the Colonel walloped and slammed away.

Twice the Professor hit boundaries with pairs of his
spectacles that had come loose in the excitement. The
Tradesmen fielders moved so far back that some of
them nearly reached their homes. Mrs Flittersnoop
was so excited she drank half a glass of paraffin, thinking it was lemonade, but not thinking so for long.

By the time the Professor and the Colonel had been got out they had more than made up the advantage which the Tradesmen had gained in the first innings. And their example seemed to have encouraged the others, for the Pagwell College Games Master made three times his previous score. The Vicar several times scored more than one run at a time. Mr Chintsbitz hit a ball so hard it was never found again. Even Maisie and Daisie, who went in giggling like anything because Mr Gardiner, the Draper, was fielding in pink and yellow braces, possibly to show he had some natty haberdashery in stock, hit six runs each in exactly the same way and were each caught out by exactly the same man.

The Tradesmen's team were three wickets down and still had fairly plenty to make when Mr Iron-monger, the Baker, was bowled one of his own penny rock cakes which had got into the bowling machine by mistake. He hit it a rousing one and it burst into showers of large crumbs. Four were caught by different people, two went into the pond and were the nearest things to ducks anyone had made in that innings. One piece hit the wicket, which instantly said 'out' five times, as if it were singing a scale, and one piece stuck to the bat.

The Pagwell Bank Manager hurriedly opened a sun-dries account and a profit and loss account. Then Mr Draper, the Blacksmith, smacked a ball wallop back into the bowling machine, right down the spout, as you might say.

Of course, Professor Branestawm's inventions couldn't be expected to stand that. They'd behaved very well up to then, but this backwards sort of bowl-ing upset the machine finally. It began to bowl special kinds of twiddley ones on its own, and the Blacksmith was out in five assorted ways before he knew what had happened.

'Out, out, out, out, OUT!' bawled the wicket gleefully.

'Toot, toot,' said the bowling machine. Zimmed up to the other end and sent down three yorkers and a daisy-cutter in a clump which disposed of Mr Pearl, the Gardener.

Three more Tradesmen were settled without so much as an eighth of a run. The radio-wickets began saying things like 'Jolly well out' and 'Out you go and stop out.' Mr Butcher, the Carpenter, was clean bowled, caught, L.B.W.'d, and stumped all at once, amid shouts of 'Outy, touty.' The bowling machine sent down batches of seven and eight balls at a time, all bouncing differently, while the Pagwell Penny Bank Manager went up in frantic fractions.

'I prote –' began Mr Fish, the Jeweller, but was hit heartily in the tummy by a ball that made him sit on his own wicket before he could finish saying 'protest'.

'Out, huffed, disqualified, revoked, miss two turns and start again,' bellowed the wickets.

'Dear me,' grunted the Professor, with his head half inside the bowling machine to see what was wrong.

'I fear this is most irregular,' murmured the Vicar, as three balls overshot the pitch and went through his larder window.

'Out, out, out, out!' yelled the wickets.

The Tradesmen sent in all their men at once, never mind whether they'd already been in or not.

Five batsmen at each wicket and one running between!

The bowling machine ran round to mid-on and

fired off a volley of balls. Then all the batsmen began to run, some round in circles as the balls had hit them, instead of the other way round.

'Hi, diddle, diddle, he's out in the middle,' sang one of the wickets.

'My goodness, by jove, sir, this must stop,' roared the Colonel, dashing into the fray.

The bowling machine bowled the Professor at him.

Then Pagwellian pandemonium raged as both teams united against the common enemy, which were the Professor's machines, and the clash of bats resounded amid shouts and squeaks of 'Out,' and roars of 'Hit it Joe,' and gasps of 'By jove, sir, what.'

The Vicar had telephoned for the police and the fire brigade, but most of them were only spare-time policemen and firemen, and were in the Tradesmen's team. Mrs Flittersnoop caught a bus to sister Aggie's with all the left-over cakes she could carry.

Then Mr Chintsbitz, smoking two cigars at once, gathered up all the onlookers, and between them they swept the tea marquee down the field and scooped the Professor's machines up into it like so many lobsters in a pot, and things were settled.

'Did we – er – win?' asked the Professor, coming out through a hole in the marquee where he had been accidentally scooped up with the machines.

But the Manager of Pagwell Penny Bank had written an enormous 'R.D.' in blue pencil on the score, which is bank language for 'Stop this nonsense,' and had gone home to count his pocket-money, which he could do easily as he had spent most of it.

6

The Great Carpet Scandal

MRS FLITTERSNOOP always took Professor Branestawm in a cup of tea of a Wednesday morning, which he sometimes tried to use for ink, sometimes poured into some chemical sorts of inventions, sometimes upset, and very occasionally drank.

'Your cup of . . . Oh my goodness gracious me, sir!'

Mrs Flittersnoop went up in shrieks, and the cup of 'oh her goodness gracious me' went most wastefully splosh on the carpet.

It was really the carpet that had shaken Mrs Flittersnoop out of her housekeeperly calm. The carpet on the walls! And the carpet on the ceiling! Yes, yes. Yards and simply yards of it. All different colours.

'Ah, there you are, Mrs Flittersnoop. A new invention of mine. How does it strike you?' said the Professor.

Just then a purple and orange rug fell off the ceiling and struck the Professor.

'Very good, sir, I'm sure,' said Mrs Flittersnoop, wondering what sort of housekeeping kind of invention the Professor thought it was.

'Liquid carpet,' said the Professor.

'Yes, indeed, sir,' said Mrs Flittersnoop.

'You keep it in a tin,' went on the Professor. 'You – er – put it on with a brush. When it dries, it – um – ah – becomes a carpet.'

'There now,' said Mrs Flittersnoop.

The Professor picked up what looked like a pot of blue jam, dipped a brush into it and painted the empty saucer Mrs Flittersnoop was still holding. The blue jam-looking stuff smoked slightly, dried off, and became a blue carpet.

'It costs rather a considerable amount at present,' said the Professor, while Mrs Flittersnoop began wondering about the cleaning, if carpets were likely to occur on all the walls and ceilings.

'But that,' went on the Professor, ' is because I have not made very much of it. When I am able to make more, it will cost less, and I am – er – hoping that in time I may be able to make so much that it will cost nothing. After that, of course, the more I can make, the more – ah – profitable it will be. You follow me, Mrs Flittersnoop?'

'Indeed, sir,' said Mrs Flittersnoop, who never followed anybody in case it wasn't polite.

Just then, a small cloud of dust drew up outside, and out of it came a small but snaky-looking motor car. Then out of the car came the Vicar of Pagwell's twin daughters, Maisie and Daisie, both dressed alike, and each with a speck of dust in the same eye.

'Professor,' they sang, both leaning through the same window, 'we're just popping along to do a spot of shopping. Care to skim along with us?'

'Oh, ah – er – thank you,' said the Professor, suddenly making up his mind to show the new liquid carpet to Mr Chintsbitz, the Manager of the Great Pagwell Furnishing Store.

But Mr Chintsbitz had a new secretary, a very brisk and bashy lady with yellow hair, who didn't agree with people seeing him much.

'He's stocktaking, you know. I doubt if he'll see you, even if you can find him,' she said, adding up dozens of tenpence ha'pennies in a book with pretty but most unbusinesslike pictures stuck on its cover.

'It'sagoodidea, cleverandconvenient,' roared Mr Chintsbitz, when the Professor at last dug him out from behind piles of furniture. But he'd had enough of the Professor's good ideas over the matter of invisible glass windows. So he headed the Professor tactfully off. 'Tell you what. Pagwell Central-Hotel. That's-erplace-for-you. Sure-to-be-interested. I'll-introduce you. Come-along.'

Mr Chintsbitz shuzzled the Professor into the biggest reddest motor car he had ever seen, and roared away through the streets with policemen saluting at every corner.

Everybody seemed to be at Pagwell Central Hotel. Mrs Flittersnoop's sister Aggie's cousin Bert's motor lorry was drawn up outside the kitchen entrance delivering considerable cabbages. Dr Mumpzanmeazle was talking to three Pagwell councillors. Maisie and Daisie were having lunch with Colonel Dedshott, and Mr Chintsbitz's secretary was having lunch with the Vicar.

Mr Chintsbitz swept the Professor rapidly through enormous rooms and colossal corridors and knocked thunderously on a small but elaborate door. The door opened and out came a small but still more elaborate gentleman with a pale face, very shiny hair, a little weeny moustache and rapidly moving hands.

'Mr Bonmonjay, meet Professor Branestawm,' boomed Mr Chintsbitz. 'Gotagoodidea. Cleverinvention. Knowyou'lllikeit. Seeyoulater. 'Bye.'

He vanished heavily down the corridor while Mr Bonmonjay, who was a Monsieur kind of Mister, began bowing politely and waving his hands courteously.

'It is a great honour to meet the so celebrated Professor,' he said. 'I have heard of the famous inventions. Ah, but yes. You will lunch with me, my dear Professor, but yes, I insist. And afterwards you shall tell me of your idea.'

'This is really most kind of you,' said the Professor

as Mr Bonmonjay escorted him to a nice little nooky corner table in the dining-room which immediately became surrounded by waiter sorts of gentlemen who scribbled furiously in little notebooks and disappeared again in all directions.

'Now, my invention,' began the Professor, but just then plates of elaborate soup arrived.

'Pardon me, my invention,' said Mr Bonmonjay, waving a polite hand at the soup.

'Excellent,' murmured the Professor. He had another go at telling Mr Monmonjay about his liquid carpet, and while he was starting to explain he lost his soup, and a rather surprised-looking little fish found itself in front of him.

'You simply brush it on,' he said, brushing off crumbs from his lap.

'Oh, la, la,' said Mr Bonmonjay, squeezing lemon vigorously over his little fish, and almost into the Professor's eyes, but not quite, thanks to plentiful pairs of spectacles.

'You will appreciate, I am sure, the – er – advantages of such an – um – ah – invention,' went on the Professor. He laid down his knife and fork to tick off some professorish calculations on his fingers, and the waiters got away with his fish, but as they left him three-quarters of a chicken in small pieces, it would have worked out none too badly if he'd had a chance to eat any.

'It can be made in all colours,' went on the Professor. Mr Bonmonjay poured out simply vases of pink lemonade, and waved his hands very talkatively.

They had pale-blue blancmange with cherries in it, which the Professor had to eat with one of his pairs of spectacles as the hotel seemed to be running short of spoons, and five sorts of cheese draped over with water-cress and little onions. But still the Professor hadn't done much explaining. Then came a basket of fruit and little skinny cups of coffee. Mr Bonmonjay lit a most exotic-smelling cigarette while the Professor gabbled off inventionary details.

'It – er – occurred to me that the idea might perhaps be of – ah – use in your hotel,' finished the Professor.

'But yes, of course,' said Mr Bonmonjay, dreamily.

Then he went quietly to sleep and gave no more trouble, while the Professor, who hadn't managed to eat much of the rather tremendous lunch, put on the wrong hat and went out through the hotel, which was now full of total strangers having polite tea . . .

Painting the liquid carpet on to the floors of Pagwell Central Hotel wasn't such an easy job as the Professor had thought it sounded. There were so many people about. And those who knew him kept asking him how he did, while those who didn't kept asking him to fetch their luggage, thinking he was a porter sort of man. And they all got most awkwardly in the way, and three times after he had carefully painted round what he thought were the legs of a piece of heavy furniture, the furniture turned out to be a heavy gentleman, and walked away leaving gaps to be filled in. But at last it was done.

Three days later a drastically urgent message arrived from Mr Bonmonjay and when the Professor got to the hotel he found Mr Bonmonjay going up in sparks and smoke all over the place and talking assorted languages so rapidly that even his waiters didn't understand him.

The Professor's carpet was all in holes. Not merely holes where furniture or people had been standing when he painted it on, but wearish sorts of holes where people had walked.

'Like paper, it wears out, so!' squealed Mr Bonmonjay. 'It is of the utmost useless. And my beautiful floors, they are ruined. What is it that I can do?'

'Hm,' said the Professor, polishing pairs of spectacles nervously and putting them in his pocket. 'There appears to – ah – be some slight disarrangement of the molecular construction of the fibres. Most unsatisfactory, and yet most interesting. One learns from these things. Yes, yes. I see what it is.' He began to get excited. 'The formula, my dear sir. That is the trouble. No provision for – er – that is, insufficient allowance for – ah – um. What is needed is – ha – I have it. Dear, dear, how very simple after all. How very simple. Yes, yes indeed.'

As he said the last words he absented himself absently and walked rapidly home, repeating figures and formulae to himself so loudly that two dear old ladies thought he was a street singer and gave him twopence.

But the Professor was on his mettle again. This wasn't the first time an invention had needed something small but important doing to it. He made more liquid carpet. And he added things. Oh yes, he certainly added things. He was determined that this lot of carpet should not wear out.

The new carpet was properly down on the floors of Pagwell Hotel, and not only in the lounges and dining-rooms, but also up the stairs, along the passages, and in the bedrooms.

Mr Bonmonjay had insisted on having painter sorts

of men in to paint it on so as to be sure of getting it done with the most thoroughness and the least mess.

A week later, the carpet showed no signs of wear. In fact it seemed, if anything, thicker and softer.

'That is but excellent,' said Mr Bonmonjay. And he took himself to lunch this time.

But if Mr Bonmonjay thought a Branestawm invention was going to lie down and give no trouble he was jolly well mistaken. In a day or two it began to be difficult to walk about the hotel. The carpet became thicker and thicker. It was growing! Actually growing!

Professor Branestawm had thought of such a brilliant idea to stop the carpet wearing out. He'd added some fertilizer sort of stuff to the liquid carpet. And just as fertilizer makes lawns grow, so it was making the carpet grow. Within a week it was a foot high.

'I reckon as we'd better mow it,' said the hotel porter.

So mow it they did, with scythes because it was too long for lawn mowers.

But mere scythes were no match for a Branestawm invention. Not they. The carpet went on growing faster than before, like a lawn does when it has been cut.

Three days later it was knee deep and harvesting kinds of men had to be fetched from West Pagwell Farm to cut it like corn, with sickles.

Two days later the carpet was waist high.

The guests began to complain. Mr Bonmonjay ran out of frantic apologies. *Pagwell Gazette* heard of it, and came out in excitable headlines saying 'Fantastic forest in hotel'.

Professor Branestawm was fetched again, and he hurried off to look up books on jungle clearance to see

if that would help. The carpet grew shoulder high, and guests began to get lost in it.

Colonel Dedshott came charging down on his horse and ploughed his way into the hotel lounge, which now had carpet almost up to the ceiling, to see if there might be some carpet tigers to be shot, but thank goodness there weren't.

Still the Professor could do nothing to stop the sensational sprouting. One determined gentleman had to cut his way out of his bedroom with nail scissors. Pagwell police said it must stop at once, but it didn't. Then the carpet came out in flower! And what flowers! A foot across, square shaped, very, very woolly, and smelling strongly of new canvas. The unheard-of blossoms peeped out of the windows of the hotel. Pagwell Horticultural Society said it wasn't fair. Professor Branestawm still struggled with carpet-abolishing preparations and nearly abolished himself.

Then quite suddenly the dreadful problem solved itself. The puzzle gave itself up. The undealable-with carpet became automatically dealt with. One merciful Monday, Pagwell Central Hotel was suddenly clear again. You could walk across the rooms with no choppers to cut away and no maps to guide you. The enormously grown-up carpet pile lay flat on the floor as if some gigantic mower had cut it.

Professor Branestawm stared studiously through his five pairs of spectacles and thought with the utmost concentration for two and a half minutes.

'Why, of course,' he said at last. 'Dear, dear, how simple. We had nothing to worry about all the time, my dear sir.'

Mr Bonmonjay made gargling noises.

'Don't you see,' the Professor began waving his hands in his explaining sort of way, 'I was so anxious to stop the carpet wearing out that I put too much fertilizer in. I exaggerated the proportions of the growing formula. That is why the growth was so – er – exceedingly rapid. I ought to have guessed.'

Mr Bonmonjay was past making noises. He could only flutter his hands about helplessly.

'And so you see,' said the Professor looking round with the air of a benevolent schoolmaster teaching twice-times tables to sweet little girls, 'the carpet outgrew its strength. The pile grew and grew until it grew right out of the foundations. Then *voilà* . . .'

Voilà reminded Mr Bonmonjay that he could speak funny languages too, and he began to do it. Waiters began to run about again. The exhausted carpet was cleared up and the place tidied. Mr Chintsbitz got a terrific order for new carpet, ungrowable, to be put down all through the hotel. And Professor Branestawm carefully wrote in his notebook some complicated particulars to the effect that if the wearing-out likeliness of carpet is attempted to be reduced by the addition of growth-producing ingredients, the proportions thereof must be carefully calculated on a basis of thickness plus time of wearing compared with the number of footsteps likely to be taken in a given area and the presumed growing power of the fertilizer employed as it applies to the constituents of the carpet.

7

The Professor Goes all Musical

To begin with, the Professor wasn't a bit musical. In fact, music was one of the reasonably ordinary things he never thought about at all. Then one day he happened to find himself in the gramophone record department of Messrs Ginnibag & Knitwoddle, in Pagwell High Street. He had been in the tool department, buying a specially twiddley kind of screwdriver, and had missed the way out, as usual. In the ordinary way he would have ambled peacefully round through stationery, games and toys, gentlemen's underwear, birdcages and fancy clocks, and come out eventually and quite accidently into Pagwell Arcade. But this time right in the middle of gramophone records a familiar sound came into his ears. It was someone speaking the peculiar language of the Diddituptite Islanders which he didn't think anybody in Pagwell understood except himself, and even he wasn't too sure of much of it.

'Hm,' said the Professor. He looked round and saw a very dark-faced gentleman in a very light suit talking very rapidly to a none too bad-looking girl behind the counter, who was talking back at him even more rapidly.

'Um, ah, excuse me,' said the Professor, raising his hat and letting fall threepennyworth of assorted screws he had put there for safety. 'I – er – know this gentleman's language. Perhaps I can be of – um – ah – assistance.'

Then there was a lot more very speedy speaking in the Diddituptite language, and the dark-faced gentleman, who wanted some records of Bangsloshly folk dances, which Messrs Ginnibag & Knitwoddle didn't see why they should stock, tried to raise his hat, but couldn't get it off as he had used gum in mistake for hair oil, and went away.

The Professor turned to the gramophone girl, and for a moment it was touch and go whether he went off into a new invention, because she was wearing a necklace made of little cogwheel-shaped pieces of stuff which reminded the Professor of whizzy sorts of machinery. But the Diddituptite language won, and they were soon deep in a considerably learned discussion on funny languages, while people began to queue up for gramophone records, and had to be served by a girl from the book department with no cogwheels round her neck, who was used to selling books so that she tried to make the people buy the records with the most words on, which wasn't the idea at all.

At last the Professor managed to get rid of himself. But he came back next day to talk to the gramophone girl again, and thought he'd better hear a few gramophone records while he was there in case it didn't seem fair to Messrs Ginnibag & Knitwoddle not to.

'How did you – ha – come to know the Diddituptite language, may I ask?' enquired the Professor in the middle of a record about somebody's sweetie.

'Well, you see,' said the girl, changing the record over for a more intellectual and less noisy one, 'my father was a big-game hunter and mother used to go with him to the Diddituptite Islands because she didn't like being left alone. And I sort of got brought up in the jungle; er – in a little house, of course, not just among the grass, you know,' she laughed.

'Um. Most interesting,' said the Professor. 'Dear, dear. Now I wonder if your father ever shot a Triddle-zonk? That is a kind of large mountain cat with square spots and three horns, you know.'

'Oh, he never shot anything,' said the girl, 'though you'd never know it to see our house, which is simply full of wild-animal skin rugs and stuffed heads. But mother bought them at auction sales, to make the place look right. Then father thought it wasn't much use try-ing to shoot anything when one could buy it ready stuffed so easily, so he gave up big-game hunting and plays the flute instead.'

She put on a flute record, and the Professor, who hadn't listened much to what she had told him, began listening a great deal to the record.

After that he gradually began to take more and more interest in music and less in funny languages, until their conversation went on almost entirely in English, and was punctuated more and more by records, a great many of which the Professor bought, but usually forgot to take home.

At last it happened. The Professor had an entirely new and world-shaking idea for new kinds of musical instruments, specially made to play a new kind of music, which he also invented as ordinary music didn't satisfy his very professorish mind, except some of the exceedingly rarefied kinds of highly wheezy music, and even they only made him feel sure he could do better himself.

The gramophone girl might perhaps have headed him back on to funny languages again if she'd known more of them, or even if she'd known more of the Professor. As it was, she got interested in his rum music and encouraged him to go on inventing, which was unnecessary really, because once the Professor began inventing no amount of encouraging could make him do it any harder, and certainly nothing short of a very wholesome bang could make him stop. And not always even that.

Mrs Flittersnoop, the Professor's housekeeper, had to keep on popping down to her sister Aggie in Lower Pagwell because, although the new inventing didn't bust the place up at all, it made considerably noisy noises, as the Professor would keep testing his instruments.

The gramophone girl found herself all caught up in the whirlwind of queer inventing and spent her evenings copying out acres of unlikely music which the Professor had invented, instead of painting sweet little pictures of coloured sparrows on fire screens, which she usually did.

Then, one day, the Professor sort of came up for breath after his inventing.

'You know, Miss – er – er – ah. These instruments of mine and this – ah – music make exceedingly instructive study, but I fear that there is – ah – not very much opportunity to make use of them. You see what I mean, my dear young lady,' he went on, polishing his five pairs of spectacles. 'One cannot – er – for instance, use these instruments to – ah – help with the housework, or – ah – solve the problems of traffic control.'

'But Professor,' said the girl, moving some expensive records which the Professor looked likely to sit on, 'you must give a concert.'

'A what?' said the Professor. He blinked at her and put all his spectacles on in a clump, but they slipped down all over his face till he looked like something in a glass jar.

'A concert, at Pagwell Town Hall, Professor,' said the girl, egging him on.

'With the Mayor and Council in attendance,' said the Professor. 'An excellent idea,' he went on. 'Yes. Excellent! I wonder if you would sell programmes?' he said, doing a bit of egging himself.

'I was hoping you would let me play one of the instruments,' said the girl. 'Just a little one, you know, that wouldn't matter much.'

'Ah!' said the Professor. 'Yes, of course. Certainly. But, oh dear, I had quite forgotten, we shall need people to play the other instruments. That makes matters rather difficult, I'm afraid.'

But it didn't make things at all difficult, because the gramophone girl had lots of brothers and sisters and friends who, it seemed, had been waiting all their lives to play the Professor's rum instruments at a concert.

Almost before he knew where he was, which he never knew very much, the Professor found himself practising his own orchestra for the concert, which the Mayor and Councillors had gladly promised to attend, guessing they wouldn't be expected to buy the instruments for making roads with or anything.

Colonel Dedshott had offered to bring plenty of Catapult Cavaliers to show people to their seats.

The Vicar's twin daughters, Maisie and Daisie, were to sell programmes and chocolates respectively.

Mrs Flittersnoop and her sister Aggie and Aggie's little girl were given free seats in the side balcony, and Mr Chintsbitz, of the Pagwell Furnishing Stores, kindly had the stage specially decorated with the most exotic curtains and rugs.

'Er, ah! Now don't be nervous, anyone,' said the Professor nervously to his orchestra on the evening of the concert, as he ran round counting the players and oiling the instruments, some of which had a decidedly threatening appearance when seen from the front.

The orchestra was not large, as orchestras go, but some of the instruments more than made up in size what the orchestra lacked in numbers.

There were four Zumpafloodles which looked something like brass violins, with two handles each, and chains instead of strings. They were played by means of small rubber mallets.

Next came the Great Woopsatara, which took three men to play it and four to hold it down.

Then there were the Major and Minor Huddabooms, which looked totally different, but both made the same noise, only one more so than the other. They were played upside down by people lying flat on their backs underneath them.

To counterbalance these, the orchestra had a series of trumpet-mouthed Twidwizzles, which had to be played five at a time to be heard at all. And a Winnibut, which looked something like a flute with a knot in it, and was played by two people, each blowing down the opposite end.

Then there was the Pedal Zonnadaisy, which was played by the feet alone, and gave imitations of almost everything. And the Big Bottleblimp, played by a man inside it who had very little to do except stay there, but that took him all his time.

The orchestra was rounded off by a Treble Contra Flattenzowl, eight feet long and fitted with a self-starter and three brakes. There was also a mouth

organ, but that had nothing to do with the Professor, and had been brought by one of the players in case he couldn't get his instrument to go.

'Nearly time to start,' said the Professor, peeping through the curtains at the clock just in time to see Mrs Flittersnoop and sister Aggie arrive. Mrs Flittersnoop waved to him and dropped her knitting which she had brought in case she didn't care for the music.

Colonel Dedshott and his Catapult Cavaliers had got all the audience into their seats in record time, chiefly by scooping them up in bunches and marching them down left right, left right, sit down, and don't ask questions.

The Mayor of Pagwell stood up to make a polite speech, and was firmly sat down again by an energetic Catapult Cavalier. At that moment the curtain went up to reveal Professor Branestawm's orchestra tastefully arranged about the stage. All dressed in their best clothes and with the gramophone girl in the centre, looking slightly fetching in a pink frock very fluffy round the shoulders.

The applause had barely died down when the Professor came on to conduct, and everyone cheered.

He was wearing his evening dress-suit which he never wore if he could help it, and had only once before put on all of it together. He felt a bit strange in it, but took heart when he looked round and saw plenty of people also in evening clothes who looked just as strange as he felt.

The Professor bowed, and his collar fell off.

'Tut, tut!' said Mrs Flittersnoop, and was just wondering whether she ought to do something about it, when the gramophone girl got up and fixed it on again for him with hair slides.

The Professor beamed at the audience, and began arranging his spectacles.

'I,' he began. 'Er – that is, we – or, perhaps – um, ah, I should say –'

'Bravo!' cried Colonel Dedshott, reckoning he ought to back the Professor a bit.

The gramophone girl put the conducting stick into the Professor's hand and hissed 'Play!'

The Professor blinked and raised his stick.

Then the music began.

The piece started with a long, drawn-out uproar from all the instruments at once, followed by separate twiddly-bits on each in turn, a good many of which were definitely on the crashy side. Then the piece got into its stride, blared and snorted like a thunderstorm in fifteen tin dustbins, swung into a frantic fizzling, and swelled up to a resounding boom and stopped suddenly. Some of the people thought that was the finish, while others probably hoped it was. But before they could get in any applause the orchestra went on again, doing much better than they had expected to. The gramophone girl sawed away at her instrument most diligently. The Professor's collar flew off again but he skewered it on his conducting stick and took no notice. Three of the players turned over two pages at once, but nobody knew. One of the lesser instruments came apart in the player's hands, but he tied it up with some string he had brought in case his braces gave out. The piece finished with a sudden zonk that shook the Town Hall's best fern out of its pot, and the applause was even more deafening than the music had been, but not much more.

Most of the people didn't like it a bit, but thought it must be very clever and applauded to show their good taste, while the others clapped so as not to be the only ones who didn't.

'Very good, I'm sure,' said Mrs Flittersnoop, passing sister Aggie some acid drops in a calico bag which she had made so as not to have papery rustlings occurring during the concert.

'Bravo!' said Colonel Dedshott, wishing he hadn't come.

The gramophone girl got the Professor put together again with more hair slides, and the second piece began.

Now, whether it was that the players hadn't practised enough, or whether they were nervous in front of an audience, or whether the Professor's instruments were a bit temperamental isn't certain. But after the first few moments it began to appear that things were not as they should be. The orchestra was swaying about in the most uncalled for manner. The gramophone girl began to get fluffy round the face as well as the shoulders. But that may have been because she had run out of hair slides.

Then the Professor's instruments definitely and absolutely got the better of the players.

The Great Woopsatara sat on the three men who were playing it and scattered the four who were trying to hold it down.

The trumpet-mouthed Twidwizzles clubbed together and put their players into a large palm-tree tub which was, fortunately, empty.

The Pedal Zonnadaisy broke out into assorted imitations, ranging from bluebottles in a jam jar to asthmatic tigers in a temper.

The man inside the Big Bottleblimp was being shot out and dropped back again in six-eight time, and the

Major and Minor Huddabooms were playing a sort of musical ping-pong with the people who ought to have been playing them.

The Zumpafloodles, the Contra Flattenzowl, the Winnibut, and the rest of the instruments were positively sweeping the floor with the musicians, and, judging by the dust they raised, it seemed as if it could do with some sweeping.

'One, two, three, four. Oh! my goodness,' gasped the Professor, doing his best to get things under control with no more hair slides to help him.

Some of the audience thought it was funny stuff put in on purpose and laughed loudly, while those in the more expensive seats tried to look as if they didn't think anything. Maisie and Daisie changed jobs, which made no difference, as they had sold all the programmes and eaten all the chocolates.

'I, dear dear. One, two, three, down, sir, stop it!' cried the Professor, still waving his stick.

The man in the Big Bottleblimp went up and down quicker and quicker. The Contra Flattenzowl began to come, threateningly, towards the Professor. The gramophone girl forgot her father used to hunt big game, and climbed up the curtains, which didn't go with the colour of her frock at all.

Then the instruments started on the audience!

Five Twidwizzles descended on the Mayor with squeaks and yelps. The Bottleblimp puffed its man up on to the curtains with the gramophone girl, and set about the people in the two and fours. The Pedal Zonnadaisy went careering up and down the gangways, giving imitations of impossible farmyards. The Zumpafloodles began climbing up to the balcony where people were still laughing, thinking they were safe.

Mrs Flittersnoop and Aggie pelted everyone indiscriminately with acid drops. The Vicar of Pagwell telephoned the Fire Brigade, but they were all at the pictures.

Crash, zoom, twiddley, twiddley, umpetty pip. Wow! 'Mind my ear!' 'Down, sir.' Zump whiz. Ooo-er!

Pandemonium raged. The gramophone girl and the Bottleblimp man dropped off the curtains on top of the Professor, who was trying to reason with the Contra Flattenzowl.

Then Colonel Dedshott got his Catapult Cavaliers marshalled in the refreshment room, and came charging down to the rescue.

Crack! Bong, twiddley, iddley weezle. Ow! Bump. 'By gad, sir.' Ta, ra, ra zoom. Wallop. 'Hurray.' Wow. Bong. Fizz. 'Dear me.' 'Take that, sir.' Oof.

Round and round the battle raged. The air was thick with noises, and dust, and acid drops. Somebody fetched a policeman, but when he saw what was happening he didn't believe it. The Pagwell Broadcasting Company, who had been broadcasting the concert, hurriedly switched off and apologized for the 'News' being late.

Crash! Wallop. 'Got you, sir.' Oo-er. Pip, pip twiddley. Ouch. Thump.

At last the Colonel and his men triumphed, and bits of vanquished instruments lay among the wreckage of the audience. The Professor and the gramophone girl sorted themselves out.

Then the audience began to ask for its money back, but luckily just then a conjurer arrived at the Town Hall by mistake, thinking it was West Pagwell School, where he was supposed to give a performance. Colonel Dedshott hurried him on to the stage, and he began rapidly producing coloured handkerchiefs, but that didn't last long as he only had four with him. Then he went on to a card trick which he couldn't do, but thought he could. But by that time the audience had quietened down, reckoning that a tame if not too good conjurer was better than a wild orchestra, and the concert managed to get itself finished without any more upheavals, except once, when the conjurer really smashed the Mayor's watch without meaning to.

But the Professor's interest in music faded quietly away after that, and although he still buys his screwdrivers from Messrs Ginnibag & Knitwoddle and occasionally calls at the gramophone record department for a few words in Diddituptite, he never listens to any records. You can hardly blame him. But the gramophone girl has a substantial piece of once-was Twidwizzle at home, hanging on the wall among the stuffed heads, just to show the family that there are more ways of being a big-game hunter than going to auction sales.

8

The Expandable House

COLONEL DEDSHOTT of the Catapult Cavaliers was
having a nice, luxurious after-dinner look at his picture post cards of famous regiments when Professor
Branestawm burst in with pairs of spectacles seeming
to be falling off every part of him as he waved a roll of
paper in his hand and scattered picture post cards of
Generals and Corporals and Demi-Sergeants most indiscriminately all over the place.

'Amazing discovery that will astonish the world,
Dedshott,' cried the Professor, flinging open the large
roll of paper, which came apart into dozens of little
rolls, and a stale bun with a bite out which the Professor had forgotten to go on with. 'Greatest invention
of our time. It will change all our ideas of – er – that is,
it will – er – ah.'

'Pah!' snorted the Colonel, shutting his post card
album just too late to stop three Captains of Mounted
Signallers from sliding into the fender.

'Listen,' said the Professor, trying to keep a very
rolled up roll of paper flat with one hand and a photo
of the Colonel's cousin Helen. 'Houses are most unsatisfactory.'

'Most,' agreed the Colonel, who was always having
to have things done to his after the Professor had
been demonstrating his rather bustable inventions in
it.

'Either,' went on the Professor, 'they have not

enough rooms for everyone likely to stay in them at one time, or if the number of rooms is sufficient adequately to accommodate the largest number of inhabitants, then it follows that when some of those inhabitants are – er – absent, the number of – ah – um – rooms becomes at once too great. You follow me, Dedshott?'

'Hm,' grunted the Colonel, still picking up post cards.

'I have invented a new kind of house which will do away with all that.' He swept his hand round and did away with four china vases. 'An expandable, adaptable, contractable, adjustable house, Dedshott. Made of an elastic material largely composed of rubber. Each room is fitted with a special valve and may be pumped up or let down according to the number of persons in the house.'

'Wonderful,' said the Colonel, feeling more at home now that his head was beginning to go round and round as it usually did when listening to the Professor describing inventions. 'Don't know how you think of these things, Branestawm. Jolly clever, what!'

'Er, not at all,' said the Professor. 'One has one's – um – ah – job to do, Dedshott. I have had constructed a specimen of my new type of adjustable house, and I was wondering if you would care to come and stay a few days in it with me. Just by way of an – ah – experiment.'

'Yes. Good idea,' said the Colonel, who had guessed something of the sort was coming, but hadn't been able to think of an excuse to get out of it, short of saying he was going to stay with his Cousin Helen, and was afraid the Professor would invite her too. And Cousin Helen in an adjustable house with let downable rooms was unthinkable. She was so unadjustable herself, as you might say, being considerably on the large side.

The next day, the Colonel arrived on his best horse at the Professor's, and found Mrs Flittersnoop, the Professor's housekeeper, busily dusting the outside of what looked like an enormous bunch of grapes on the lawn.

'Ha, there you are, Dedshott,' said the Professor's voice, and the Professor himself burst silently out of a door in the bunch of grapes. 'Here you see my new adjustable house. The rooms are somewhat ball-shaped because it is so difficult to make anything blow-upable a square shape, owing to the corners becoming de-cornered in the inflating process.'

'Amazing,' said the Colonel, who wasn't listening much, as he didn't want his head to start going round, because his horse was already going round by itself, and he had all he could do to get off it at the right time and place.

'It is all very simple and convenient,' said the Professor, showing the Colonel round his excessively round house. 'The motor which carries the house in its folded condition generates heat for cooking and light for – er – er –'

'Lighting,' said the Colonel, not seeing what else it could be for.

'Precisely, Dedshott. These' – the Professor pointed to a number of sticking-out parts, which made the bunch-of-grapes-looking house look as if the stalks were growing on the wrong end of the grapes – 'these are the pumping up and letting down valves. Supposing, for instance, that we do not require this particular bedroom. We simply unscrew the valve cap and *voilà*!'

It wasn't so much *voilà* as we-e-e-e-e-e-p-zug, as the not-wanted room went down like ten bicycle tyres with none too slow punctures, and the escaping air blew the Colonel's hat off in spite of its being held on with elastic; a military precaution against being de-hatted which he had learned from a picture post card of a Mountain Musketeer.

'The rooms have double walls,' went on the Professor, taking no notice. 'The air is pumped between the thicknesses; but that is not all, Dedshott. My house, being made from a material largely composed of rubber to make it – er – stretchable, is also weatherproof. In winter it prevents the warmth from getting out and in summer it stops the heat from getting in. A most desirable arrangement.'

They went inside, and Mrs Flittersnoop served them a most appropriate dinner consisting of an omelette, which began by being enormously large but gradually shrank down to a very skinny fried egg looking one as it cooled. It was made from a recipe the Professor had invented, and it should have been fastened down with drawing-pins until needed.

At last it was bedtime.

'Here is your room, Dedshott, said the Professor, pointing to something that looked like many mackintoshes in a mound.

'Allow me!' He pulled an elastic lever and puff, puff, puff, woof, the mackintosh-looking mound expanded into a bedroom all done out in pink pansies and with the Colonel's initials embroidered on the ceiling, which was a little surprise Mrs Flittersnoop had prepared.

Next morning the Colonel woke up in a bush.

'Pah!' he growled. 'Confound these invented sort of

houses of Branestawm's. Something unusual gone wrong as usual I suppose.'

But actually, nothing had gone wrong and it wasn't the Professor's fault that he was so out in the open. The Colonel's horse, which he had tied to a disused croquet hoop, had got away and bitten off the Colonel's room, thinking it was some kind of horsey sort of food. Then, of course, the Colonel's bedroom had gone very wizzily down, z-z-z-z-z-m. Goodness knows what would have happened to the Colonel. He might easily have been smothered with his own initials as the ceiling came down, but luckily for him he was no end of a one for fresh air, and he'd left his bedroom window wide open. So when the room went down, it simply squeezed him gently but firmly out of the window like so much tooth paste out of a tube.

Breakfast was only half over before the Professor began pulling elastic levers and twiddling adaptable valves. Air puffed in and zizzed out with noises ranging from that of ten impatient trains leaving Pagwell Junction in a bunch to that of one weary pussycat leaving some dinner he didn't care for. Finally the Professor let the whole house down into a fairly generous-sized heap of folded sort of flollops, rolled it into a motor van kindly lent by Mrs Flittersnoop's sister Aggie's Bert, who, as a rule, used it for carrying such things as coals or vegetables, or children to picnics, and was obliging the Professor for the day.

'Well, Branestawm, I must say you've excelled yourself this time. My word, yes, you know, what!' said the Colonel, deciding to say no more about being squeezed out of the window. 'Most clever idea. Highly useful for soldiers and all that, you know. Better than tents, handier than barracks, and more comfortable than bivouacs, by jove. My friend, the General, must see this, Branestawm.'

'Er, yes, yes, of course,' said the Professor. 'But the – er – fact is, Dedshott, I have already promised it in a way to the Pagwell Council, who are coming to see it tomorrow.'

'Pah!' snorted the Colonel, who didn't care much for the Pagwell Council as they kept making him pay rates for things he didn't agree with. 'I'll bring the General here tomorrow. Meet Pagwell Council, confound them, and we shall see, yes, by jove, sir.' And with a flourishing salute to Mrs Flittersnoop, who nearly fell over a clothes basket in trying to curtsey back again, the Colonel was gone.

Then the Professor got his house off Bert's van, pumped up the kitchen in mistakes for a bedroom, and went to sleep in the sink.

Professor Branestawm's expandable house was blown up to its uttermost utmost. The Mayor of Pagwell and several important members of the Council were being entertained to tea and house-blowing demonstrations. So was Colonel Dedshott's General and one or two of the General's Assistant-Generals and decorative Majors. Mrs Flittersnoop and her sister Aggie and sister Aggie's little girl were serving tea, which they had made secretly behind a bush outside, as sister Aggie wasn't too sure if she agreed with collapsible kitchens.

'You see, gentlemen, my invention is all, and more, I – er – claim it to – um – ah – be,' said the Professor, looking round through all sorts of pairs of spectacles.

'Marvellous,' grunted Colonel Dedshott, taking another piece of seed cake as the General had been eating off his plate by mistake.

It was a severely separated and definitely disconnected kind of tea party, because no one room of the house would hold all the imposing people at one go. So some of them were in the dining-room, some in the lounge. Colonel Dedshott, his General, and his General's friends sat in neat military rows in various bedrooms. The Mayor of Pagwell sat in state in the bath, propped up with cushions. And the Professor, who had left all the doors open to make polite conversation easy, if none too simple, owing to talking round corners so to speak, sat nowhere at all, but ran about spilling tea into umbrella stands.

'Certainly, certainly,' said the General, passing the
Colonel's cup for more tea and taking a bite out of a
tart belonging to a Major. 'Say no more about it, Professor. We approve the idea entirely. Yes, indeed. Just
what the army wants, sir. Every man carries his own
house. Movable barracks, my word. What do you say,
Dedshott?'

'Marvellous,' agreed the Colonel, picking up the
General's cup, but the General had already emptied it.

'What about drains?' asked the Pagwell Councillor
who saw to inspecting sanitary sorts of things.

'Negotiations for securing the proposition will commence forthwith,' said the General, borrowing an Assistant-General's pencil.

'Wait a minute there, not so fast,' said the Pagwell Councillor in charge of streets and houses. 'This is not a military idea at all, sir. I want streets of these houses laid out in Pagwell for the winter, then in summer, as people go for holidays, the houses can be de – er – de – er – let down, folded up and deposited at the Town Hall until required.'

'Thus leaving additional space for recreation grounds and playing fields,' put in the Pagwell Councillor who looked after sports and pastimes.

'Nation's defence comes before nation's convenience, sir!' shouted the General, leaning forward to talk round into the dining-room, which didn't help, as the Councillors were on the piano in the drawing-room. 'Have the kindness to withdraw, sir.'

'What about drains?' said the Sanitary Councillor again.

'Another cup of tea, sir?' said Mrs Flittersnoop, taking his cup and handing it to sister Aggie, who poured out no end of hot water, as she'd forgotten to put tea in the pot.

'No – er – drains are necessary, I assure you,' said the Professor, 'though it would, I fear, take rather long to – ah – explain why.'

'Hear, hear,' said a Pagwell Councillor, whose own drains had gone wrong at home.

'Confound it, sir, this is no mere matter of drains!' shouted the General. 'Safety of nation may be at stake. Do you hear, sir? Safety of nation. And you talk about drains. Pah! Yes sir, pah!'

'Perhaps we had – er – better see what the – ah –

Mayor has to say,' suggested the Professor, blinking about a bit as things began to get arguish.

But the Mayor had gone to sleep in the bath and was dreaming that the rates had gone up to double.

The arguments grew fiercer and noisier. The house swayed with the thumping of fists and bouncing of bodies inside it. Suddenly Mrs Flittersnoop gave a shriek.

'Oh my goodness, sir, indeed. Look, sir, look, if we aren't blowing away, sir, oh dear, dear!' she screamed.

The Professor looked out of the window. Oo-er! the blow-upable house had broken from its foundations owing to the bashing about inside. The wind had caught it and was blowing it up in a way the Professor had never intended. A queer balloon, sailing high above the tree-tops.

That stopped the argument. Partly because the General didn't want soldiers who might go up in the air at a moment's notice, partly because the streets and houses Councillor didn't want houses that might run away with people before the rent could be collected. But most of all because they were all too scared about being up in the air to do any more arguing.

'Keep calm, keep calm,' said the Professor, getting frightfully flurried. 'I will open some of the valves and we shall descend gently.'

'No, no!' cried Colonel Dedshott, who had no wish to be squeezed tooth-paste fashion out of windows hundreds of feet up in the air. 'Rooms will collapse, by jove, yes, sir. Pull levers, Branestawm. Twiddle those wheel things. Confound it, sir, pull levers, pull levers!'

But, alas! Lever pulling was no use this time. No! It was a case of open valves and be squeezed out high above the tree-tops or leave them closed and be blown goodness knows where.

Suddenly, there was the most exaggeratedly explosive kind of pop, like three hundred pounds worth of penny balloons being busted at once. The next second the Professor's house was in bits of various sizes which were flying off at various angles, while the Professor, the Colonel, the Councillors, Generals, and Mayor were falling in a heap with the wind whistling past their eyebrows.

Sister Aggie's little girl had done it. Yes, she had. She'd tried to fix a calendar on the expandable kitchen wall with a pin. A pin, mind you, in a blown-up inflatable house. Oo-er! No wonder the bang and the bits!

Down they shot, and whizzed, and whistled, and dropped. Pagwell Canal glinted beneath them like a silver ribbon with tucks in it. Very pretty! But who notices pretty things when they're falling into them? Down, down down! But ha! Thank goodness a barge happened to be passing along the canal. And the barge was full of straw being delivered to the Camel's Back Brick Factory. They landed with a series of soft plonks into the straw. Very undignified, but no more so than landing in the water, and ever so much drier. But the Mayor was missing from the straw-landers. A little way off, though, there was a noticeable splash ; the Mayor had landed in the canal. He was in the bath, but no longer asleep. The bath acted as a boat. Luckily the plug was in and kept the water out instead of keeping it in as bath plugs usually do.

The Mayor seized a back-scrubbing brush and paddled himself along. And he enjoyed it so much that they had rather a job to get him to come out.

And that was almost the end of the Professor's

expandable house. But not quite. For the pieces were picked up in various places by various people who used them as make-do mackintoshes and temporary umbrellas and meantime sponge bags, according to what sort of people they were ; while the Professor brought his idea down a bit small and made an expandable meat safe which could be blown up on Saturday, ready for Sunday's joint, and gradually let down as the week passed through the stages of cold joint, warmed-up joint, stew, hash, soup, and cat's dinner. But of course, one had to be careful of skewers.

9

The Gurglesome Noises

I T was Mrs Flittersnoop, the Professor's housekeeper, who first heard the noises. But for some time she didn't take any notice. Because, as she told her sister Aggie afterwards, 'I said to myself, there now, that'll be the Professor at his inventing again. Not but what the noise wasn't exasperating, as you might say, and me a day behind with my ironing, but there, I was never one to complain.'

'B-r-r-r-r-r-awm-m-m-m-ong-ng-ng!' The zooming, booming noises sounded like someone playing a bad-tempered organ, without bothering to use any but the deep-down notes.

'Mrs Flittersnoop,' came the Professor's voice. 'Mrs Flittersnoop. Will you please get that cat in or drive that dog away, or turn the wireless off if it's on, or on if it's off, or – er – stop frying sausages with the door open, or whatever it is that is making that noise. I'm trying to write a most important letter, and the disturbance is most – er –is most – er – disturbing.'

Then he went back to his study to try to finish his important letter, but found he couldn't finish it because he hadn't begun it. He'd forgotten that it wasn't writing an important letter, but reading a book about undiscovered alphabets, that the noise had interrupted.

'Begging your pardon, sir, I'm sure,' said Mrs Flittersnoop, coming in with the iron in one hand, 'but I thought the noise was you, sir.'

'Tut, tut, Mrs Flittersnoop,' said the Professor. 'How can a noise be me? If you have studied Wattawun's *Theory of Sound and Individuality* which I lent you last week, you should know that a noise as such is impersonal.'

'Yes, sir. Indeed, sir,' answered Mrs Flittersnoop, who had borrowed Wattawun's *Theory* to press some flowers in because it was a generously weighty book. She hadn't read a word of it, possibly because it was written in Latin, which was Greek to her. She'd often heard the Professor spoken of in Pagwell as a big noise, but didn't see how he could be as he was a rather little man.

'Ha. Hum – er – very strange, but possibly interesting,' said the Professor, putting on his five pairs of spectacles that he'd been using as book-markers, and losing all his places.

Zooooooom. Bim, bim, bim, bim. Aw-m-m. Bong, bong, bong, zoom! The noise went on. 'It's ghosts!' gasped Mrs Flittersnoop. 'The place is haunted, sir, that it is. Full of those evil spirits it'll be, and which I never could abide, sir!' She gave a shriek of her own. She dropped her iron on the floor, where it began to burn a carefully shaped hole in the carpet on top of another hole of quite another shape that was already there. She shot out of the front door bang into the arms of Colonel Dedshott, who was looking for the bell, but couldn't find it, as the Professor had shifted it to the other side to make room for an automatic boot wiper.

At last they all got themselves sorted out, which wasn't too easy, as Mrs Flittersnoop was rather caught up on the Colonel's medals.

They searched the house for whatever was making the noise. The Professor and the Colonel found each other four times when they weren't expecting to, and nearly did something nasty to each other, but, fortunately, neither of them could think of anything nasty to do in time. Mrs Flittersnoop shut herself in the airing cupboard and hoped for the best. But, oo–er – the noises suddenly sounded loud and terrifying, close beside her.

'Ow. Help, sir! Ghosts, sir, help!' she screamed. She tried to burst out of the cupboard, but the Professor had mended the latch, and she was fastened in. She beat frantically on the door and shook next week's clean sheets down on herself.

'Ha. What's that?' cried the Colonel. 'More noises coming from this way.'

'Um, well, now we shall know what is causing the disturbance,' said the Professor. He opened the cupboard. A flapping white thing darted out, uttering muffled shrieks, and the zooming noise sounded even louder. 'Spooks!' grasped the Colonel.

It was now the Professor's turn to shriek. But before he had time to do it the sheets fell off and Mrs Flittersnoop collapsed with considerable creaking into a none too new wicker chair.

But the Professor had found out what the noises were about. The water-pipes were gurgling and vibrating with a booming drone, like second-hand aeroplanes in distress.

'Well, thank goodness for that, I'm sure,' gasped Mrs Flittersnoop, when they'd made her a cup of cocoa to revive her, which it did all too rapidly, as the Professor had given the Colonel a tin of knife polish to make it with.

'Hum, now let me see,' murmured the Professor, poking about among the pipes, tapping on the tank, and looking into the loft. 'We must get this noise stopped.'

They certainly must, but they couldn't. The Professor tried fixing things round the pipes, and bending the pipes both towards each other and away from each other. He wedged things under places, and he scraped things from on top of places. He managed to start a small leak, but he couldn't stop the loud noises.

The Colonel tried shaking the pipes and rapping out commands. But the pipes were definitely not military pipes, and the noise went on. Mrs Flittersnoop tried turning the taps on and off one at a time, and in various groups, but all she managed to do was to splash considerable water on the gas-cooker, where it immediately sizzed itself up very rapidly into steam.

'Tut, tut, we must go to the Water Company about it,' said the Professor.

But it was early-closing day at the Water Company, so they had to wait till next day. The noise went on energetically all night, and neither the Professor nor Mrs Flittersnoop could get a wink of sleep.

Next day, round went the Professor to the Water Company, and they sent a plumber kind of person along.

'Ah!' said the plumber, 'I can see what's wrong here. The water-pipes are making a noise. That's what they're doing.' Then he went away to get an assistant plumber.

'That's a nasty noise,' said the assistant plumber.

'Something wrong with the pipes,' said the head plumber.

Then they both went away for tools, and when they got back it was time to go away for dinner.

After dinner they began trying to stop the zooming noises the pipes were making by making excessively banging and hammering noises themselves. But the zooming became, if anything, louder than ever.

And where the previous night the Professor and Mrs Flittersnoop hadn't been able to sleep a wink for the noise, this time they were kept awake the whole night by the row.

'Bother these water-pipe sort of contrivances,' said the Professor. 'Why can't we have water delivered in bottles twice a day, like the milk? I shall speak seriously to the Water Company.'

Then the Water Company sent an extra-special sort of Lord Chief Plumber, in a peaked cap with gold braid, who actually managed to stop the noise, by will-power or something. But it began again as soon as he took his eyes off the pipes. So he tried leaving a very stern photo of himself, taken when he was in the navy, propped up opposite the pipes. But the noises broke out again, in several places.

'Dear, dear. I can see I shall have to deal with this myself,' muttered the Professor. He pulled out several yards of apparently unemployed pipe till it hung, like disappointed macaroni, in stiff festoons about the place. He carefully unscrewed a highly important-looking tap, but, unfortunately, he had forgotten to turn off an exceedingly more highly important tap somewhere else. Suddenly, there was a noise like rough sea in a forest. His-s-s-s-s, swoosh, fiz-z-z! Enough nice, clean water to bath all the babies in West Pagwell came suddenly out of everywhere at once. It washed the Professor rapidly away. Water gushed splendidly

down the stairs. It spouted happily through the
banisters and round the umbrella stand. Heavy
showers descended in joyous squirts through cracks in
the ceiling. Never had domesticated water had such a
time. And it was making the most of the chance. It
would show Professors that being measured in distilled
doses into tuppenny test tubes wasn't the only thing
water was fit for. Deputy Niagaras foamed over the
window-sills. Artificial oceans swelled across floors.

'Mrs Flittersnoop, quick!' cried the Professor, flinging himself upon a tea tray and paddling feverishly
with a wooden spoon. 'Mrs Flittersnoop, give me
something to wrap round the – flwoof – pipes.' He blew
out a mouthful of wild water that had gone in for a
look round.

Mrs Flittersnoop had been making pastry, but now she was on the mantlepiece because she didn't think mixed paddling was right. The Professor saw the pastry, grabbed up a sheet of it and struggled up streaming stairs, using the tea tray as an umbrella.

A rather young Water Company man arrived on a bicycle, gave one look at the tumbling torrents, and went hurriedly away to be a Coal Company's man or something else dry.

At last the Professor managed to swaddle the pipes up with Mrs Flittersnoop's pastry and stop the wetness. But still noise hummed, and droned, and zoomed. Still the Professor couldn't sleep much, and Mrs Flittersnoop was kept awake almost entirely. She would have gone to stay with her sister Aggie, but her sister Aggie was suffering from drains in the house, and had gone to stay with her cousin Sybil. The Professor would have gone to stay with Colonel Dedshott, but the Colonel had got a bit particular about having his house invented to bits, and he made extensive excuses.

'Really this is dreadful. I – ah – don't know what can be done,' murmured the Professor, 'which is most strange, because as a rule I know at once what can be done, even though I must – ah – admit that sometimes it is something which it is impossible to do.'

He began to get so sleepy that if he got into a bus it was certain to cost him at least two pink tickets and a long blue one instead of an ordinary penny white one.

Once he fell asleep in the middle of giving a lecture at the Pagwell College, which wasn't so disastrous as it might have been, as all the audience were already asleep themselves, except an eyeglass-making sort of man, who was hoping the Professor might break some of his pairs of spectacles so that he could sell him some new ones.

Mrs Flittersnoop dozed off, and let three poached eggs go hard boiled, while the water for the tea would have been burnt if it could have been.

The zooming noises went on as loudly as ever, and, in addition, there was sometimes a very cookish-pastry kind of smell that seemed nearly as loud, but which was due to some of the pipes the Professor had wrapped the pastry round being hot water sort of pipes, which were making a kind of pie of the job which the Professor had already made somewhat of a hash of.

Then the pastry began to crack off, and Mrs Flittersnoop had to give up four pairs of her thick, woollen stockings to help stop the water bursting out again, which seems rather unfair on her. But she didn't mind, because she was able to knit herself six more pairs on a special machine the Professor had invented for tieing up parcels, but which worked much better knitting stockings. Anyway, Mrs Flittersnoop wasn't one to complain. She'd even have lent one of her thick, woollen vests, only it didn't seem ladylike.

At last the Professor gave up trying to stop the noises, and started work on an invention for a special kind of elaborate night-cap which would make it possible to go to sleep, never mind how much noise was being made, or by who, or what for, or where.

When he got the first model finished, he put it on to see if it worked.

'Hum – er – wonderful!' he said. 'Highly successful. At the first attempt, too. Most creditable. Clever of me, I must say.'

Not a sound could he hear. With the special night-cap on the zooming noises were shut completely out.

'Well, well, well. Now who says Professors can't do things?' he muttered. Nobody said so, because nobody was there. But they might have done if they had been there, for when the Professor took the night-cap off he found the zooming noises had jolly well stopped!

Yes. Yes. Not a boom, or half a clang, or the smallest portion of whizzes, bims or zims could be heard.

'Er my, dear me. Most extraordinary, to be sure,' said the Professor. 'Can my invention be more successful than I had hoped? Surely not. How can inventing a night-cap stop water-pipes from making noises?'

Goodness knows how the noises had managed to get themselves stopped. Were the pipes tired of being fiddled with and pulled out or pushed in, according to what sort of pipes they were? Or didn't they like pastry, or couldn't they stand thick, woollen stockings, or had the Water Company sent some secret plumbers round without saying anything? Anyway, there it was, and quietness reigned at last where water had rained not so long ago.

'So you've stopped the noise at last then, sir, have you?' said Mrs Flittersnoop. 'Well, I must say I'm not sorry to hear it, sir, if you understand what I mean. Not that I wish it to be thought that I'm making a fuss about what has to be, sir, but I shall be glad to hear the last of it, and that's the truth.'

But, dear, dear! Neither the Professor nor Mrs Flittersnoop could sleep a wink. No. No. They couldn't. The noises had been going on for so long that they'd gradually got used to hearing them, so that they didn't keep them awake much any more.

But, now, dear! dear! tut! tut! With the noises stopped, they found it as hard to sleep as they had when the noises first began. The absence of noises seemed louder than the noises had been. The booming had become so soothing, they couldn't get to sleep without it.

'Er – um – ah – oh –, very strange, I'm sure,' said the Professor. 'I can't understand it ; though I probably shall be able to when I've remembered which book to look it up in.' He thought for a bit, and suddenly he had an idea. A proper Branestawm idea it was.

'If we've got used to sleeping with the noise, and we can't sleep without it,' he said, 'the only thing to do is to have the noise back!'

What! Make the water-pipes start zooming and humming and bonging all over again, after all the trouble it had been to stop them? Yes, yes. That was the idea. But it was none too simple an idea to carry out. For if it had been difficult to stop the noises, it was abso-jolly-well-lutely the dickens of a lot more difficult to start them again.

Water Company men came and went. The Chief Plumber gentleman brought his photo round upside down, and glared at the pipes till his eyeballs nearly fell out. But only silence rewarded his efforts, which was no reward at all for a man who wanted noise.

Mrs Flittersnoop offered two of her second-best shawls and a basin full of new cake mixture for applying to the pipes, but they did no good.

Colonel Dedshott brought several Catapult Cavaliers round, and between them they managed to drink a lot of water out of the pipes, generously mixed up with other things. And they managed to start plenty of noise among themselves with old Catapultonian songs. But not a whisper did they get from the pipes.

'Er – um. Most annoying,' mumbled the Professor.

Then he had another idea. And if the last idea had been a Branestawm sort of idea, this was even more so, if possible.

'I shall have to invent a special kind of machine to make noises like the water-pipes used to make, so that we can get some sleep,' he said.

And that was what he did. He had to have a good many tries before he got the noise machine right. First it was too high, and Mrs Flittersnoop overslept herself, while the Professor didn't sleep at all. Then it was too low, and the Professor overslept himself, but Mrs Flittersnoop woke up every five minutes for four and a half minutes each time. Then it was too poppety, and not zoomy enough. Then it was plentifully zoomy, but there were not enough whizzes. At last it was perfect and the Professor used up seven and a half previously inadequate inventions intended for planting pansies ten at a time, for keeping neckties from curling the wrong way, for peeling onions without making you cry, and doing other possibly useful things, which they didn't do.

But the noises went on, and the Professor was able to sleep again. Mrs Flittersnoop wasn't kept awake at night. And everything was all right, except that the neighbours complained of the row. But by slow degrees the Professor managed to make his noise machine make gradually less and less noise, so that in the course of a considerable time he was able to sleep peacefully without disturbing the neighbours.

But he never dreamed any really good ideas for inventions without forgetting them just as he woke up.

10

The Pagwell Motor Race

FLAGS hung in the streets of all the Pagwells. The paths were black with people, and the roads were yellow with sand. There was to be a motor race. Yes, there absolutely was. And the prize was a magnificent silver cup presented by the Mayor. It was really a slightly enormous cake basket his grandma had given him plenty of years ago, turned upside down and with some of the ornamental bits taken off and fixed on somewhere else.

But what was perhaps the most excitable feature of all was the fact that first on the list of entries for the open race was 'Pagwell Pride,' the splendid and sensational invention of none other than Professor Branestawm.

Colonel Dedshott was going to be the Professor's mechanic sort of person, and go with him in the car.

'Most people,' said the Professor, explaining the invention to the Colonel, 'imagine that speed is merely a matter of going quickly.'

'Ha, yes, of course,' said the Colonel, not taking any too much notice of what the Professor was saying, because he was waiting for his head to start going round and round, which it never failed to do once the Professor really got going with an explanation.

'Actually, my dear Dedshott,' went on the Professor, polishing his five pairs of spectacles with five differently coloured pieces of cloth smeared with five different spectacle polishing pastes of his own invention. 'Actually, it is a great deal more than that. Speed is a relative matter concerning time and distance, but we must not forget the force of gravity.'

'No, no,' said the Colonel, and he sat down on a chair which the Professor had just moved somewhere else, so he landed a considerably jangly bump on the floor ; medals and all.

'If,' went on the Professor, beginning to put the five pieces of coloured cloth on different parts of his face, and trying to crumple the five pairs of spectacles into a ball, which they didn't lend themselves to very well – 'if we reduce the ratio of time and increase the ratio of distance without – er – er – without affecting the proportionate gravitational resistance, the result is clear.'

'Absolutely, what!' said the Colonel, struggling to his feet.

'So the greater extent to which we are able to do this, the greater will be our speed,' gabbled the Professor. 'And as there is no limit to anything which is relative, there is, consequently, no limit to our speed.'

'Jolly clever, what, my word, yes,' said the Colonel, heartily taking the Professor's word for about seven-eighths of it, which he hadn't understood at all. 'Upon my word, Branestawm, I'm beginning to feel sorry for those other chaps in the race, you know.'

'Oh well – er – the – er – scientific mind, Dedshott, is bound to – er – um – ah – triumph in the end,' murmured the Professor. Then they went out to get the car ready for the race, while Mrs Flittersnoop, the Professor's housekeeper, put on her best bonnet and went to collect her sister Aggie and her sister Aggie's little girl from Lower Pagwell, because they all had very special seats reserved for them by the Professor on the balcony of Great Pagwell Town Hall, right opposite the starting and finishing place.

The cars were lined up. In addition to Professor Branestawm's 'Pagwell Pride,' there was 'Flying Fanny' belonging to the Ice Cream Man. There was 'Roaring Scarlet,' which was, as a matter of fact, the Great Pagwell fire engine, driven by the Chief Fireman, who fancied he knew something about speed through going to fires unmentionably rapidly. The Pagwell & District Motor Transport Company had entered a very excitably luxurious motor 'bus sort of charabanc they'd just bought, the fares on which were going to be double the ordinary bus fares as it had no advertisements on the outside, which was supposed to make it look considerably more genteel.

Dr Mumpzanmeazle, who was used to dashing off in all directions very suddenly when people became urgently ill, thought he might as well dash off rapidly in one direction and possibly win a prize for it. But he had his little black bag in case of anything.

Then there were the twin daughters of the Vicar of Pagwell, each driving a little weeny, but very saucy three-wheeled sort of car, painted pale blue. If either of them won the race things looked like being awkward, because nobody could tell which of them was which, not even the Vicar himself who told by the shape of her ears which was Maisie, but as a matter of fact, that one was Daisie.

'Well, they've got a nice day for it, I'm sure,' said Mrs Flittersnoop, changing seats with her sister Aggie for the fifth time so that Aggie's little girl could see better. 'And I must say I do hope as the Professor wins.

Not that I hold with all this rushing about in motors, as you might say, Aggie, but –' At that moment they all had to change seats again because they had the wrong ones.

'Attend please!' cried the Assistant Mayor, ringing a large bell he had borrowed from Upper Pagwell High School. But he only gave it four dings and three dongs when the clapper flew out and landed with rather a squish in nine-penny worth of eggs somebody had with them, but whether to take them home or throw them at the competitors isn't certain.

'Listen to the rules of the race,' sang out the Assistant Mayor. Some of the rules were quite easy sort of rules, like 'First car past the winning-post is the winner,' but some of them were excessively twisted up and complicated sort of puzzle find the answer rules, such as 'Any competitor arriving at or passing the winning-post, either not under his own power or lacking more than three-quarters of the parts of his vehicle, shall be deemed to be disqualified, providing he shall not, within a hundred yards of the post, have been obstructed by another competitor similarly lacking, but this rule shall be held to be void if the first-mentioned competitor shall show, to the satisfaction of the judges, that such lack was caused prior to or during the third lap unless otherwise stated elsewhere.' There were also a few special rules like 'No competitor shall wear a red waistcoat,' which had been put in because the Mayor didn't think competitors should be allowed to do as they liked.

'Are you all ready, Dedshott?' whispered the Professor nervously, peering about in his car with one pair of spectacles after another. 'Really, this racing business is most disconcerting. Most discon – er – certing. The

most difficut part of a race seems to be before it starts. Interesting, but – ah – um – puzzling.'

'Ha!' said Colonel Dedshott, who had himself all keyed up as if he was going into battle, and wishing there was more room for his legs.

Mrs Flittersnoop waved respectfully to the Professor, but the Assistant Mayor thought she was waving at him, and turned his nose up slightly, to show her that official sort of people mustn't be waved at.

But. Oh! Goodness, the Professor had his car facing the wrong way. Oh dear! dear! But nobody knew it was facing the wrong way. Not that both ends looked alike, because they looked drastically different. But it was imposible to tell which was the front as the Professor and the Colonel sat in the middle, back to back, and facing sideways. The Assistant Mayor was getting ready to start the race. The Professor would go the wrong way, and there was no rule to say what was to be done about that.

Suddenly, there was a bang, and three of the cars

shot off, but had to come back again because it wasn't the start, but only Mrs Flittersnoop's sister Aggie's little girl's balloon, which had busted itself on her Auntie's hatpin. Then the Assistant Mayor raised the starting-pistol and pressed the trigger. But nothing happened because he'd forgotten to load it.

The Professor got out of his car to give it a drop of special oil in a difficult to get at place, and only got half back into it when the Assistant Mayor managed really and truly to start the race by bursting five shillings worth of balloons all at once, that a balloon man was selling just beside him.

Off shot the cars! Clouds of dust rose in the air! Assorted smells occurred! Shouts went up! The Professor's car was first away. But, being only half back in his seat, he started it backwards by mistake. Thank goodness for that, because he was facing the wrong way, so now he went the right way, but the wrong way round, which didn't matter, as nobody knew. The Vicar's twins' hats both blew off at exactly the same moment. The Pagwell Transport Company's 'bus took the first corner with half its wheels in the air, which was possibly just as well, as one of them had fallen off. Part of the Professor's car fell off, but that was all right, as he'd put in some extra parts to be on the safe side.

Whr-r-r-r- pop, pop, bang, whizz, puff, hurray, wow, whiz-z-z, 'Good old Branestawm,' 'Go it, Maisie,' chugugugugug, bang, pop, atishoo, 'Bravo, Doctor,' whr-r-r, bangety clank, pop, 'Firemen for ever, hurray,' pouff, went the cars and the dust, and the people cheering, and the people sneezing because of the dust, and the people making faces because of the smell. Round the first bend, down the dip, over Pag-

well Bridge, past the Gasworks, and out of sight on the first lap.

Mrs Flittersnoop undid one of the many packets of sandwiches she had brought, because she thought it wasn't much use being a housekeeper if you couldn't be well sandwiched.

'Really, most invigorating, not to say instructive,'

said the Professor, fiddling with levers as they shot along, and wearing all his five pairs of spectacles in a clump to act as sort of goggles, which they didn't do, anything to speak of.

'Ha,' grunted the Colonel, who had his mouth and eyes so full of rushing air he couldn't say much and didn't want to say anything.

Then the Professor caught sight of what he thought was a new kind of cow with hardly any legs, but which was really the usual kind of cow standing in a puddle. And before he knew what was happening he'd turned left instead of right. Oo–er! the left turning led straight into the Pagwell Canal. In another seven and a quarter seconds the car, the Professor, and the Colonel would be in considerably more of a puddle than the cow. Thank goodness, the Colonel lost his nerve for a moment, and threw up his hands. His elbow caught a lever. The car stopped suddenly without slowing down and instantly began going rapidly back the other way. Out of the left turning it shot, and into the right one, just as the Ice Cream Man and the Fireman came tearing up side by side. There was a loud crash, and everything was all of a goodness knows what. The three vehicles were all tangled up together, and all of them stopped, except the Professor's. On it went, right end first now, because of the backwards sort of reversing it had done a moment before. And on with it, thank goodness in the right direction, but one sideways and one cornerways went the fire engine and 'Flying Fanny,' closely followed by Dr Mumpzanmeazle, who kept feeling he ought to do something about the tangled-up cars, but he couldn't catch up with them to do it.

On they surged, and popped and whirred and

clanked and bumped, through Lower Pagwell and West Pagwell and Pagwell Docks and Pagwell Gardens.

'Push them off, Dedshott. Push them off. Remember rule fifteen,' gabbled the Professor, remembering rule eleven and thinking it was fifteen, but as it was the one about not wearing red waistcoats it made no difference.

'Ha! My word, you know. Get off. Play fair you fellows, what!' cried the Colonel, trying to push the other cars off with one hand and hang on to the Professor's car with the other.

They took a corner so sharply that they took a small helping of fence with them as well, and the next moment they were pounding past the Town Hall and starting on the second lap..

'Bravo, Professor, I'm sure!' cried Mrs Flittersnoop, not understanding motor races, and thinking the Professor was wonderful to have captured two of the others already.

Opposite the Gasworks the Ice Cream Man's car came unstuck from the pile and dropped with a rattle into the road, where it was immediately run into by Doctor Mumpzanmeazle, and the Ice Cream Man began an argument about the Doctor's having to buy one as he'd stopped him or something.

Mrs Flittersnoop opened another packet of sandwiches and changed seats with her sister Aggie.

'By jove, Branestawm, we're winning, you know!' shouted the Colonel, beginning to get a bit used to things and managing to dislodge the fire engine, which blew out a shower of sparks and made straight for the cow that was still standing in the same puddle.

'Y-e-e-e-es!' shouted the Professor, twiddling wheels

and pulling levers like anything without making the slightest difference. 'Most creditable performance, though I say it myself, Dedshott. The ratio of time to distance, as I remarked before –'

There was an extra loud whiz, and the Vicar's twins shot by, one on each side. Both smiled exactly the same sort of smile and disappeared both at once into an excessively ample and prickly bush at the side of the road, through not looking too accurately where they were going.

'Accident!' cried the Colonel. 'Forward the Cavaliers.'

The Professor stopped the car, but didn't trouble to get out as it stopped so suddenly that both he and the Colonel were shot out, and landed in the bush along with the twins.

'Er – er – er, allow me,' said the Professor, trying to raise his hat, but not succeeding, as it had blown off.

'Trust you – puff – not seriously – puff – puff – hurt,' panted the Colonel.

While they were rapidly and politely getting Maisie and Daisie out of the bush, and getting themselves severely into it so that Maisie and Daisie had to get them out of it, by shot the motor 'bus, with two wheels missing and one on inside-out, followed by the Doctor and the Ice Cream Man, still arguing.

'On with the race, what!' roared the Colonel. Maisie got into Daisie's car, and Daisie into Maisie's, which didn't notice, but may have muddled things or not. Both of them had the same sort of scratches from the prickly bush in exactly the same places, some of which didn't show.

Past the Town Hall again. Third lap. Twins leading by half an inch. Professor next. Then the Ice Cream

Man and the Doctor. The motor 'bus had stopped for new wheels, but couldn't find any the right size.

'Are you enjoying it, Aggie?' said Mrs Flittersnoop, opening more sandwiches which fell to bits as she got the paper off, as she hadn't put enough butter on to stick them properly.

Suddenly the cheers changed to howls of amazement. Down the road was galloping a delighted-looking cow with muddy legs, drawing the fire engine backwards with the Fireman clinging on with all the arms and legs he had, and wishing he had more.

Whir-r-r-r, pop, bang, wallop, 'Hurray,' whiz.

Two broadcasting sort of men who had been trying to make a running commentary gave up and turned on some dance music. The Assistant Mayor forgot how many laps there were to be and couldn't get through the crowd to cross the road to the Town Hall and look it up. So he started making signals. Mrs Flittersnoop thought he was being friendly, and threw him a packet of sandwiches, which landed on the Vicar's hat and burst all over him in a shower of breadcrumbs and not-quite-sufficiently-hard-boiled egg.

Now there seemed to be an extra sort of someone in the race. But it wasn't a racing sort of someone. It was someone who wanted to catch up with Dr Mumpzanmeazle, because some other someone had caught an illness.

Pop, bang, whir, 'Hurray,' crash, wallop. The Professor passed the twins. The Ice Cream Man passed the Professor. The Assistant Mayor found he had notes about the race in his waistcoat pocket ; discovered there was only one more lap to go, and had the winning-post tape stretched across the road. But it wouldn't reach, so he had to tie his braces to the end of it and fix his trousers up with safety-pins, which made him feel slightly like Professor Branestawm, whose coat was always fastened with safety-pins.

Mrs Flittersnoop ran out of sandwiches, and changed seats with sister Aggie again.

'My word, Branestawm, last lap. Winning-post, what!' gasped the Colonel as they shot round the last bend.

'Most gratifying. Most gratifying,' said the Professor. Then seven separate parts of his machine fell out, and it stopped. 'Dear me. Now why did that happen, I wonder?' said the Professor, testily. 'Most annoying. I'm afraid this racing business is more complicated than I thought. Oh dear! Where is that little square cogwheel?' The Professor began frantically scooping up bits of motor car. Not far behind the twins had stopped to powder their noses, both with the same kind of powder. The Doctor had been caught up with and hustled away to see about some spots someone had come out in.

The cow with muddy legs had dragged the fire engine into a wet field and was trying to eat it. The Ice Cream Man was stuck in the ditch. It looked as if the race would never end, because there was nobody left to win.

But, oo-er, the motor 'bus had found some almost suitable wheels, and it was thundering up. The 'bus driver still believed that speed was only a matter of going quickly. So unscientific.

'The ratio of time to distance is increasing, I fear,' gabbled the Professor, hastily stuffing pieces of fallen-off machine back into the car.

Colonel Dedshott grabbed the bottle of lemonade Mrs Flittersnoop had made up for them, and emptied it into the fuel tank, like a silly. But the Professor had brought the paraffin by mistake, as Mrs Flittersnoop kept it in the same sort of bottle. Suddenly the car started again. The Professor fell in upside down. The Colonel ran behind. Whiz-z-z-z. Evidently it liked paraffin, for it did several hundred miles per hour for thirty-one yards. Then the paraffin gave out. The Colonel jumped in and tried to get the Professor unstuck. The motor 'bus thundered round the bend and bore down on them. 'Quick! Ha. Do something, what!' gasped the Colonel.

'Toot, toot, zum, zum, pop,' said the motor 'bus.

'Er – um. Most unusual,' came the Professor's voice, very muffled, from among the machinery.

The motor 'bus would pass them in another second. And only a few yards to go.

Suddenly, there was a most resounding bong. The motor 'bus had caught up with the Professor. But it didn't pass him. No. No. It ran jolly well into him. Bang! wallop! 'Oo-er. My word, Branestawm, what!'

'Tut, tut, I fear this is most – er –'

The motor 'bus stopped, but the Professor's car started. The 'bus batted it along for ten yards, and at the ninth yard the Professor's engine found a drop more of Mrs Flittersnoop's paraffin it hadn't noticed before. With a whiz and a roar the Professor and the Colonel shot past the winning-post two inches ahead of the twins who had just come tearing up. The Professor's car hit the tape. But the tape was plentifully too strong for a winning-post tape, and it didn't break. The Assistant Mayor's braces broke instead. Then the Professor's car fell to bits, and the Colonel and the Professor crawled triumphantly out of the pieces that lay in a neat pile like steaming tea leaves.

Professor Branestawm had won the race after all. The Mayor presented him with the silver cake basket sort of cup and was glad to see the last of it. The Professor gave it to Mrs Flittersnoop, who passed it on to her sister Aggie, but burglars stole it and sold it to another someone who sent it to his cousin who gave it to her great-aunt who happened to be the Mayor's grandma. And she wanted to know a considerable deal about how the Mayor came to part with it.

Still. The Professor won the race, so what else mattered?

11

Fire! Fire! Fire!

Mrs Flittersnoop opened the kitchen door, then she slammed it to again and went shrieking along the passage.

'Oh, Professor, sir! Quick, quick! Oh, indeed, sir! Help! Oh dear!'

She dashed up the stairs to look for the Professor.

She was no sooner out of sight than the Professor came out of his study and opened the kitchen door. And he, too, slammed it again and went tearing along the passage.

'Mrs Flittersnoop! Dear me, where are you, Mrs Flittersnoop? Oh! this is dreadful. Dear, dear!'

He dashed up the stairs and met Mrs Flittersnoop on the landing, where they both began jabbering rapidly at each other, and couldn't understand what each other were saying. But as they were both trying to drag each other down to the kitchen, they succeeded plentifully well.

For the third time the kitchen door was opened. And this time out came considerable smoke. Flames were flickering up to the ceiling. Crackling noises were going on. There were sparks.

A piece of coal had shot out of the fire and set light to a pair of the Professor's pyjamas which were airing on a clothes airer of his own invention. And whether the Professor wore exceptionally burnable pyjamas, or whether the coal was extra eager to please as the

coal merchant was a friend of the Professor's, there
was no end of a bonfirish sort of flare up.

'Help! sir. Quick! Water!' squealed Mrs Flittersnoop. She dashed through the smoke to the sink and
began to throw bowls of water at the flames. Only as
she picked up the colander by mistake for a bowl,
nothing much happened, not even steam.

'Oh, my goodness! Tut, tut,' spluttered the Professor. He tried to smother the flames with a rug, but
the rug burned rather better than his pyjamas. He
snatched up a bottle of Mrs Flittersnoop's home-made
banana wine and emptied it on the flames. But that
only made them change from yellow to green.

Mrs Flittersnoop dropped the colander and started
to drag the burning things outside. But the Professor
had thought of the same idea, and they dragged each
other outside, treading in the cat's saucer of milk as
they went.

If only Colonel Dedshott had been there. He would
have had the flames out in no time. He'd have lined
them up and marched them into a bucket of water or
something. Or blown them out with no end of military commands. But Colonel Dedshott was away
having a few days' holiday.

If only some of Mrs Flittersnoop's firemen friends
had been there, they'd have made short work of the
fire. But they were down at the fire station waiting for
fire alarms to ring.

Mrs Flittersnoop ran shrieking to the garden shed
for the hose, and got herself tangled up in it like a
bluebottle in the macaroni.

The Professor rushed up the street looking for the
fire alarms that Mrs Flittersnoop's friends were waiting
to hear go off. He found what he thought was a fire

alarm, smashed the glass, and pulled the handle. But it was a talkie weighing machine. It said, 'Three thousand, four hundred and eighty stone, two ounces,' in a very rapid voice and clapped twenty-two cards in the Professor's hands, each bearing next month's date and a bit of fortune-telling talk, which said that the Professor should beware of a dark man with fair trousers.

'Tut, tut! Help! Fire!' shouted the Professor. He flung the cards up in a shower like butterflies and rushed on. He smashed the fronts of two red penny-in-the-slot chocolate machines and tore on, leaving dozens of boys of all sizes scrambling for the chocolate. He bashed open a little box fixed to a lamp-post, in case it would bring a fire engine. But it brought the Pagwell motor ambulance. Still hunting frantically for fire alarms, the Professor smashed three clocks, one of them two hours fast, which made no difference; two barometer sort of things for telling you what sort of weather it probably wouldn't be; and some very special traffic lights that the Pagwell Council thought rather highly of. Then he collapsed, all out of breath, into the barrow of an old-iron man, who knew him rather well, through having called for some of his used-up inventions, and wheeled him carefully home.

Meantime, flames rose higher and higher. A wax model of the Mayor of Pagwell disappeared into yellow gravy with a soft hiss. Mrs Flittersnoop's spotted muslin curtains went pouff and couldn't be spotted at all. Then the fire reached the gas meter and, bong! Seven and sixpence worth of best gas, all ready counted out in therms, went most extravagantly off and blew a corner off the hot-water tank. Three weeks' washing-up water came slosh out of the tank in a lump and the fire was out, just as the Professor arrived in the old barrow, which was fortunate for the old-iron man, because of the gas meter and all that.

'It really seems to me, Mrs – er – Flittersnoop, that the question of fire alarms is one to which I should – um – give attention,' said the Professor, later.

'Yes, sir, indeed, that I'm sure,' said Mrs Flittersnoop, busily frying sausages over an oil stove in the Professor's study, as the kitchen was still suffering from the fire.

'I had not realized that fire alarms were so very – ah – difficult to find until I tried to find one myself,' went on the Professor.

'Like pillar-boxes, sir, if I might make so bold as to say so,' put in his housekeeper, placing a plate of sausages and mashed potatoes at the Professor's elbow. 'Why, I remember my sister Aggie going out to post a letter to her George while she was spending a few days with her cousin Kate –'

'Er – of course, of course,' said the Professor hurriedly, before Mrs Flittersnoop made still more bold and got on to her sister's little girl's hair that couldn't be made to curl. 'Now my idea is a radio-active fire alarm in every district, that will, immediately upon a fire starting in its – er – vicinity, set off an alarm at the nearest fire station. Automatic, you see. The human element eliminated.' He speared a sausage on the end of his pen, looked at it absently, shook it off into the waste-paper basket, and began filling an envelope addressed to the Pagwell Gas Company with mashed potato.

'Very clever, I'm sure, sir,' said Mrs Flittersnoop, who hadn't been listening much, because she was making the Professor a cup of coffee and herself a cup of tea, both out of the same kettle to save space, 'though I can't say I hold with too many of them things myself, because I always say it's better to go straight to the Post Office than waste time looking for a pillar-box that mayn't be there, so to speak, sir.'

But the Professor was too busy munching some last week's sandwiches he'd found in his pocket to answer. Then he put on his hat, the right way round and the proper way up, both of which were unusual for him, and went to see the Pagwell Council about his wireless fire alarms.

'We have never had anything like this before,' said the representative of Lower Pagwell doubtfully, after the Professor had explained his idea and all their heads had finished going round and round with listening to so much professorish talk.

'For my part, I don't think it will work,' said the West Pagwell man, who was new to the place and didn't know yet that, with the Professor's inventions, it wasn't so much a question of their not working as of their working too much.

'Fire is a serious matter, and it ought to be prevented,' said the Upper Pagwell man, who loved preventing things so much that he'd nearly prevented there being any Pagwell Council.

'But gentlemen,' said the Professor, getting all worked up, and fishing about for stray spectacles. 'This invention of mine will be a boon to – er – civilization. We shall be able to sleep and go about our business without fire of fear – er – um – tut, tut! I mean – er – that is – It is the best thing I have done since – er – since – hum, let me see now, what is it the best thing I've done since?'

'Ah!' said the Pagwell Docks man, who always went

to his business without fear of fire because it had to do with generous quantities of ice.

At last the Council agreed to let the Professor put up just one Branestawm Fire Alarm to see what it could do. Then there was some discussion as to where it was to be put. Each of the Members of the Council wanted it outside his own house, because, although they didn't believe it would be much use, they thought it would be handy to have it there in case it was. Except the Vicar of Pagwell, who already had one ordinary fire alarm, a pillar-box, a telegraph pole, a lamp-post, a sand bin, and a telephone call-box in a clump outside his gate, and felt that was enough for one person, and possibly too many for a Vicar, though he wasn't sure why.

Finally, the fire alarm was fixed outside the entrance to Pagwell Common, so that a bonfire could be lit on the common to see if it worked.

The Mayor himself lit the bonfire, very ceremoniously, and got his eye very unceremoniously full of smoke, owing to wind and all that.

'I don't believe it will work,' said the West Pagwell man. 'Ought to be prevented,' mumbled the Upper Pagwell man. 'Ah!' said Pagwell Docks.

'Dear me! I hope I haven't left out any of those little, tiny screws that one leaves out so easily,' murmured the Professor, clashing his five pairs of spectacles together nervously. 'I'm not sure if I used enough wire, either.' As a matter of fact he'd used all the wire in Pagwell, except what was already being used for fences, sweet-pea guards, telephones, and clothes lines, which ought to have been plenty for a wireless fire alarm. But one never knew. Not with Branestawm inventions, one didn't.

The bonfire crackled up like ten Guy Fawkes days. The smell was awful, because of someone's old goloshes that had got in by mistake. The fire alarm made no sound.

'I knew it wouldn't work,' snorted West Pagwell, lighting a pipe that made the smell worse, only it didn't notice.

Then, clang-a-ling-a-lang! Whizz! Puff, puff, clang! Ziz! Crash! Ow! The Pagwell Gardens fire engine suddenly arrived with all the firemen in their best clothes and wearing carnations in their button-holes because they'd been waiting specially for this call and wanted to look a bit special themselves.

Of course, that settled the question. Even West Pagwell had nothing to say against the Professor's fire alarm after that.

So Professor Branestawm disappeared into a specially extensive Inventory that the Pagwell Council lent him, which was really East Pagwell Baths made nice and dry, to get positively no end of his special wireless fire alarms made. And the Pagwell Council, who believed in doing things thoroughly, also kindly lent the Professor rows upon rows of slightly engineerish sort of men. Some from the lamp-post works, some from the tram car machinery seeing to department, some from the steam-roller weighing rooms, and even one or two from the Great Pagwell Museum.

'Um! Well, this is certainly a very generous way of doing things, I must say,' said the Professor, who had so many assistants that all he could find to do himself was sit in one of the little undressing boxes at the edge of the once-was swimming bath, and polish his five pairs of spectacles on a towel marked 'P.B.', which meant Pagwell Baths, and not Professor Branestawm, as you might expect.

The Pagwell Post Office got themselves all interested in the work, possibly because fire alarms are the same colour as pillar-boxes, and obtained special permission from somewhere dreadfully important to present the Professor with a pot of red paint for the fire alarms.

The Associated Bakers' Society, Pagwell Section, sent a special mould for putting the words 'fire alarm' in ornamental birthday cake letters on the fire alarms, and made it a little stronger than usual so that it could be used for cast iron instead of cake icing.

The Pagwell Broadcasting Station sent two very nicely spoken gentlemen along to see that everything was all right about oscillations and broadcastery matters of that sort.

Mrs Flittersnoop went to stay with her sister Aggie

in Lower Pagwell, but they both called at the new Inventory every day to bring the Professor's dinner. And they usually had an absolute time of it trying to find the Professor, for he had taken to using undressing boxes as offices, and studies, and thinking rooms, and nobody could ever be sure which of the dozens of them he was in. Besides which, there were some rather awkward notices about, marked 'Gentlemen's Swimming Bath,' 'Gents' Dressing Rooms,' and so on. And although these of course didn't count while the baths were being used as an Inventory, Mrs Flittersoop and her sister Aggie were a bit on the nervous side about notices, and used to find it rather difficult to get about the place.

Colonel Dedshott, who had heard of things from the Professor, and managed to understand the letter by reading it backwards and upside down both at once, sent a very military telegram or two of encouragement, and someone, who thought himself probably no end of a funny one, sent a picture post card of a comic fireman, on which he had drawn five pairs of spectacles.

At last the Branestawm Wireless Fire Alarms were all finished and fixed up all over the Pagwells. The Professor sat in his study trying to fill up no end of forms that the Pagwell Council thought it might be slightly jolly to have filled up. Mrs Flittersnoop was cooking roast beef, new potatoes, and peas, golden syrup pudding, and jam tart on a special oil stove the Professor had invented for cooking all those things as he was getting tired of sausages, and the kitchen wasn't ready to be a kitchen again just yet. The Pagwell Gas Company were being difficult about their busted gas meter, which had been rather a favourite of theirs. And they were a bit cross about the envelope full of mashed potatoes the Professor had sent them in mistake for the money for his gas bill.

'Well, Mrs Flittersnoop,' said the Professor, putting his name on a form which really wanted to know where he lived. 'These fire alarms are a very satisfactory business. My work is all over Pagwell. My name will go down to – er – Where is it that names go down to, Mrs Flittersnoop?'

'Down to the sea in ships, is it, sir?' asked Mrs Flittersnoop, who was busy with the roast beef.

At that moment the Pagwell fire engine shot past with a whirr and a clang, and the Professor raced Mrs Flittersnoop to the window by three inches and a knocked over vase, to wave to them.

'Excellent, excellent!' said the Professor, rubbing his hands together as soon as he'd finished using them for waving. 'I had not expected results from my fire alarms so soon.'

But it wasn't quite so excellent after all, because when the fire engine arrived on the spot the only fire they could find was one someone had just lit in their fireplace. No sooner had they discovered that than another fire alarm, right at the other side, by Pagwell Gardens, rang its bell at the Fire Station. And as they hadn't a spare engine, they had to send the grocer's boy on his bicycle right over to Great Pagwell for the other one.

But bother it all, the Pagwell Gardens fire was a bonfire in the Vicar's garden, and before the engine even got there two more alarms went off, one from Pagwell Docks and one from Upper Pagwell, one of which turned out to be the Mayor of Pagwell lighting a rather lavish cigar close to a fire alarm, and the other was set off accidentally by the Pagwell Council's drain-watching department, who had some men with a little fire in a bucket digging the road up.

The Pagwell fire engine dashed recklessly in all directions. The grocer's boy had to get all his old school friends to help him catch it as new alarms went off here, there and nearly everywhere.

One of the fire alarms got tuned in to the B.B.C. by mistake, and played lots of Henry Hall without a licence, until a steam roller ran into it.

The Pagwell Council sent a frantic message for the Professor to go round and see them about things.

'Dear dear me! Most annoying!' he muttered. 'There is nothing wrong with my fire alarms,' he said when the Council told him about the awkward alarms and the false fires. 'It is merely that I have made them too – er – sensitive. They record with unfailing – um – accuracy the slightest indication of fire. Really, gentlemen – um, ah – I don't think you can exactly blame me.'

Fire alarms went off in North Pagwell, Pagwell Hill, and Pagwell Twittering, a village near South Pagwell, consisting of one cottage, three churches, and a pond. All kitchen and dining-room fires. A haystack caught fire near East Pagwell, and the fire alarm there burst.

'I knew it wouldn't work. Said so from the start,' growled the West Pagwell man.

'But it does work, it does work, don't you see!' cried the Professor, waving spectacles about and upsetting the ink. 'It works, but it works too well! It must be adjusted so as to record only conflagrations of a major order.'

Five fire alarms that had already gone off before went off again. The fire engine wore its wheels out, and the hose and ladders had to be pulled off and packed inside a red motor 'bus, borrowed as a sort of deputy fire engine.

'No, no, no!' protested the Pagwell Council, knowing what the Professor's adjustments were likely to do. 'Take them away. Never had them before. Better without them.'

Colonel Dedshott, arriving home from his holiday in full uniform, was mistaken for a very special kind of fireman, and hurried off on an ice-cream tricycle to an alarm caused by somebody's hot-water bottle.

Then Professor Branestawm's own house caught fire while Mrs Flittersnoop was out waving to the firemen. The Professor's special oil stove had done it. And no wonder. Cooking roast beef and golden syrup pudding on an oil stove, indeed.

But, oh dear! Good gracious, and help! The firemen had got so tired of rushing round after futile fires and questionable conflagrations, that they'd gone back to the Fire Station to make a cup of tea. And they took no notice of the alarms. They thought the Professor's actual and serious house on fire was another false alarm. Yes, they did. Until Colonel Dedshott and Mrs Flittersnoop came rushing in, hand in hand, to gasp out the awful news. And by then the house was nearly in cinders.

'Oh dear! I wish I'd never thought about fire alarms,' groaned the Professor. 'I might have guessed something awful would happen, but I'm no good at guessing. Now what shall I do? No Inventory left. The Pagwell Council will not be willing, I fear, to lend me the Baths again. No, I feel sure they will not. In fact, I have to collect all the wireless fire alarms I put in for them. Most distressing.'

'Don't worry, sir,' said Mrs Flittersnoop. 'If it's somewhere to stay you want, why, my sister Aggie will give you a room, and be pleased to do it, that I'm sure. I shall be staying there myself till things are put to rights, and between us we ought to be able to look after you, sir.'

There was nothing else for it. The Professor went to stay with sister Aggie, at Lower Pagwell, while his house was built again, and sister Aggie let him have the bicycle shed as a sort of make-do Inventory.

Colonel Dedshott was so furious at being mistaken for a fireman, that he went away again at once for another holiday.

And all the wireless fire alarms the Professor had to take back from the Pagwell Council. What about those? Well, he found that, although they were a shade too conscientious as fire alarms, they made very pleasant little wireless sets. So he gave them to Pagwell Hospital, where their being painted red fitted in very well. The only thing was, they had to be kept warm, or they didn't work. But the hospital managed that beautifully, by having a weeny gas ring under each one.

That pleased the Gas Company, who forgave the Professor for busting the meter and sending mashed potatoes, and promised him an extra large, fancy sort of meter when his house was ready.

And Professor Branestawm achieved the really astounding distinction of being the first man to invent a wireless set that worked by gas.

12

The Professor Stays with Sister Aggie

OF course, Mrs Flittersnoop, the Professor's house-keeper, frequently went to stay with her sister Aggie, in Lower Pagwell. She went whenever the Professor's inventions rather busted the place up, which was none too seldom.

But this time, what with a special oil stove the Professor had invented setting fire to his house while he was out, and on top of that, his too conscientious wireless fire alarms getting the Pagwell Fire Brigade all muddled up, the Professor's house was more than usually drastically done for and not liveable-in. So the Professor had gone with Mrs Flittersnoop to stay with sister Aggie.

'Come along in, sir. I'm only too pleased to have you,' said Aggie. And in the Professor was hustled, fussed around, clothes brushed, spectacles arranged in the wrong order, and sat in an arm-chair that was considerably more comfortable than it looked. Then Mrs Flittersnoop and sister Aggie disappeared into the kitchen and there began the noises of cups of things being got ready, and plenty of arranging sort of talk, so as to give the Professor the best bedroom, which looked out on Lower Pagwell High Street, with trams going slowly and clankily by very frequently when you wanted to get to sleep, but very rarely when you were waiting for one.

Next morning the Professor was awakened at half-

past five by sister Aggie's husband, who drove one of the better-class trams, going out by the back door so as not to spoil the front step. And later on by the sounds of sister Aggie's little girl being got ready for school, which seemed to take plenty of time, and which sounded rather like lots and lots of children being got ready to go to the seaside for a fortnight.

'Um!' said the Professor, picking his five pairs of spectacles carefully off the brass bedrail where he'd hung them the night before so as to be tidy in someone else's house.

He was just going to start making out an invention on the wall paper when there came a tap on the door and sister Aggie brought in a cup of tea.

'I didn't bring it before so as not to disturb you,' she beamed. She let up the blinds with a crash. 'I always think it is nice to have a bit of a sleep in the first morning in a strange bed.'

When she had gone the Professor stacked his spectacles carefully on his nose, and sipped his tea. But oh dear! Sister Aggie was so hasty and hearty in her way of doing things she'd slopped positively quantities of tea in the saucer. And it dropped off the bottom of the cup, right splash on the best counterpane that sister Aggie's grandma had embroidered with her own hands.

'Tut, tut, most careless of me,' muttered the Professor, thinking the mess was his fault, which it wasn't for a change. 'Dear, dear, what will Mrs – er – Aggie think of me?' He put the cup and saucer down beside him and began very earnestly rubbing at the tea-stained counterpane with the sleeve of his pyjamas. This made very little difference to the stain, but it knocked over the cup of tea, slosh! all over the best pillow with lace trimming made by sister Aggie's cousin Mabel's own hands.

'Oh! my goodness. How very careless of me,' wailed the Professor. 'I – er – really – er – this is most – er – It places me in a most awkward position.'

Thank goodness Mrs Flittersnoop took it into her head to come up with another cup of tea very neatly set out on a small, round tray with a paper whatsname under it, and not a spot spilled. Knowing what her sister Aggie was with cups of things.

Shattering noises were coming from the bicycle shed sister Aggie had let Professor Branestawm use as a make-do Inventory. It contained no bicycles, but it was considerably stacked-up with portions of old mangle, spare bits of old pram, finished-with kettles, collapsed sewing machines, once-new wheelbarrows, and other drastically dealt with domestic machinery.

Professor Branestawm didn't mind. He liked to have plenty of odd cogwheels about. He was never really happy without quantities of disjointed works. He thoroughly enjoyed a few unintentional spokes.

He was inventing a special unsloppable cup and saucer, particularly for the benefit of sister Aggie and other hearty but none too steady-handed people.

'Liquid will always find its own level,' said the Professor, remembering something he had learned at school. 'But the question is this. Is the level that belongs to tea the same level as that which is the property of cocoa? And if so, how do they manage about it when they both find it together? Hum! perhaps that may account in some way for the extreme sloppability of some liquids.'

The Professor put a pair of pliers on his nose in

mistake for one of his pairs of spectacles and began again at the beginning.

He invented seven different sorts of cups that wouldn't slop blanc-mange, or treacle, or stiff honey. But they all positively did slop anything more runny if handled carelessly. He tried making them different shapes, which caused them to look most rum and unteacup like, but made them no less spillable.

At last the Professor lost his temper.

'Ridiculous!' he cried. 'Here am I, Theophilus Branestawm, inventor, master of mechanics, doctor of dynamics, and goodness knows what, unable to invent a merely special teacup. Pah! I never heard of such a thing. Didn't I invent a special spring-cleaning machine?' (My word he did.) 'Didn't I invent a never-stop clock, even though it did burst? Wasn't I responsible, through my pancake-making machine, for there being round paving stones instead of square ones in Pagwell? What about Branestawm's non-shine glass, and Branestawm's burglar catcher, and Branestawm's — pah! What are mere teacups?' The Professor certainly had his mad up. Just to show himself what was what, he invented a reversible mangle with shirt-shining attachment; a thing for getting the pips out of, and the skin off, grapes, while still leaving some grape. An automatic egg skinner, and an elastically driven brace-button replacer.

'Now!' he grunted. 'What about that unspillable teacup?' Either the Professor's rapid bit of inventing had sort of warmed-up his brains, or else the idea he was waiting for was waiting for him, and got impatient. Anyway, all of a sudden, *voilà*. There was the perfect, unspillable teacup. In three designs (all of them awful, but never mind).

'Mrs Flittersnoop,' he cried, dashing out with the cups and arriving in the coal cellar instead of the kitchen because he'd forgotten it was sister Aggie's house he was at.

He filled the unspillable cups with tea specially made for the occasion, and Mrs Flittersnoop, sister Aggie, and sister Aggie's little girl had a go at trying to slop the tea out of them.

They couldn't do it. They ran carelessly upstairs. They shot even more carelessly downstairs. They tripped over the mat, both intentionally and otherwise. They slipped down the banisters. But not one quarter of a drop of tea did they manage to spill.

'Very good, I'm sure, sir,' said Mrs Flittersnoop, and sister Aggie said, 'What will they think of next?'

'We must celebrate,' said the Professor. He dashed off with the still unspilled cups to make an enormous unspillable tea service, and to send invitations for a tremendous tea-party.

Professor Branestawm's tea-party in Pagwell Town Hall was to be a very lady-like, balance your cup on one knee sort of drawing-room kind of tea, because the Vicar's wife had kindly offered to help with the arrangements, and she was rather a one for being polite. Otherwise, Mrs Flittersnoop would have had what she called a good, sensible, sit-down meal, which meant you could eat more without appearing rude. Tea was being served from a long table full of the Professor's unspillable cups and a number of plates of rather pale, home-made gingerbread, kindly given by sister Aggie, who wasn't as good at gingerbread as she thought she was. On the platform at the end of the hall, at a table with bigger cups and thinner gingerbread, sat the Mayor of Pagwell, who was going to make a speech if he got half a chance ; Professor Branestawm, because it was his party ; Colonel Dedshott, in case the Professor needed a bit of backing-up ; the Vicar of Pagwell, because his wife had done some of the arranging ; and Mr Bakewell Skoneligh, of the Pagwell Bakeries, because he had sent the tea-making apparatus and wanted to keep an eye on it.

Mrs Flittersnoop and sister Aggie poured out the tea into the Professor's unspillable cups, and everyone stood about waiting for someone to start first.

'Hum – er – ah – er – hum!' said the Professor, wondering if he ought to say something. But the Mayor and the Vicar both stood up together and said 'Ladies and Gentlemen,' then they looked at each other and sat down again, the Vicar on a piece of gingerbread the Professor had absently put on his chair. So the Mayor, who hadn't sat on any gingerbread, took advantage of his advantage, so to speak, and spoke.

'Ladies and Gentlemen,' he said, 'it gives me great pleasuah to be here today on this notable and, perhaps I may say, auspicious occasion.'

'Bravo!' said Colonel Dedshott, and everyone applauded.

'To drink the first drop as it were,' went on the Mayor, 'from Professor Branestawm's un – er – un – un –' 'Spillable,' murmured the Professor. 'Teacups,' finished the Mayor.

There was more applause, while the Mayor lifted his cup to his mouth very correctly, little finger sticking out and all. Presently he put it down again and there was a slight look of surprise on his face. He looked at the Professor, who was looking at a Town Hall spider on the ceiling and didn't see him. He

lifted his cup again and appeared to be trying, in as polite a way as possible, to eat it.

The Vicar lifted his cup. And his little finger stuck out even further than the Mayor's because he was even more used to polite tea-parties.

Everyone else lifted their cups. Little fingers stuck out all over the place. The Professor beamed on everyone and forgot about his own cup of tea.

'How nice to have an invention that gives no

trouble,' he thought. 'Nothing can go wrong this time. There are no cogwheels that I might have missed out. No levers to get pulled the wrong way. No super-differentials to slip – Good gracious!'

Good gracious it certainly was. The polite tea-party was going through the most unusual convulsions. Everyone seemed to be trying to get inside his teacup. Necks wriggled. Eyes bulged. Heads waggled.

Oh, Professor Branestawm! Oh, those unspillable cups! Unspillable they certainly were. The Professor had made them unspillable by having a sort of turned-in lip round the edge, and so as to make absolutely unspillably sure, he'd put a fairly generous lip round Alas! the result was that although not a drop could possibly be spilt from the cups, neither could a drop possibly be drunk from them.

The Vicar had another piece of gingerbread and hoped for the best. Colonel Dedshott frowned into his cup and wondered if smashing it would be any use. The Mayor of Pagwell kept smiling vacantly and raising and lowering his cup, trying to pretend everything was quite all right.

'The principle on which these – er – cups are constructed,' said the Professor, thinking perhaps he might make everyone forget about their tea if he talked sufficient complications at them.

At that moment, little Willie Wibbelspeck, cousin of Mr Bakewell Skoneligh, the baker, fished out of his pocket a rather bent drinking straw, stuck one end in his unspillable cup of undrinkable tea and drank it up, rather impolitely, but completely successfully.

'Ha!' said Colonel Dedshott. He had a few rapid whispery words with Mr Bakewell Skoneligh who vanished out of a side door while the Colonel got up and said, 'Er, ha, what! This reminds me of an experience I had when I was in the tropics, by jove, yes.' And he began to tell them a very long, drawn-out, military kind of un-joke about mosquitoes, but, fortunately, he was only about two-thirds through it when the baker returned with an armful of drinking straws which he managed to get hurriedly passed round. So the party managed to finish up drinking rather cold sort of tea through straws, which was all right except when a tea-leaf stuck in a straw, which it frequently did.

'Well! never mind, sir, it was very clever, I'm sure,' said Mrs Flittersnoop afterwards. And the Professor didn't mind so much because he'd just heard that his own house would be ready to move back to on Friday.

Next morning, sister Aggie brought him up a cup of tea as usual, in an ordinary cup, with exactly three-sevenths of it slopped in the saucer. So the Professor poured the rest out of the cup and drank it all out of the saucer, with no finger sticking out and the trams clattering past as loudly as ever.

Branestawm's Bomb

PROFESSOR BRANESTAWM fixed the last screw into place in his latest invention and then, picking it up very carefully because it was a definitely explosive sort of invention and rather liable to make a bust up of things if dealt with casually, he carried it gingerly from his Inventory to his study.

'Mrs Flittersnoop,' he called to his housekeeper. 'Bring me some wrapping-up paper and string and stuff for doing up parcels, and an old cardboard box if there is one.'

He put the invention down on his desk when it instantly fell apart, leaving the supposed-to-be-inside all exposed and considerably much of the rest of it all over the place, for although he had very carefully remembered to put in the last screw properly, there were several exceedingly necessary earlier-on screws, as you might say, that he'd overlooked because he'd been so anxious to get the invention finished.

'Oh! dear me, very careless, I'm sure,' he muttered.

By the time the Professor had gone back to his Inventory, got the new machine properly put together again as to its middle screws and remembered to stop himself going on with rather several other inventions he had partly invented, Mrs Flittersnoop had brought in plenty of paper, ample string, and four old cardboard boxes, two of which were so old as to be hardly boxes and very nearly no longer cardboard and one of which was full of two of her old hats that she'd put away in case a man at the door might one day offer her a fern or so for them.

'Thank you, thank you, that is excellent,' said the Professor and began making a sort of a kind of a parcel of his invention while Mrs Flittersnoop went back to the kitchen to cook him an egg for his tea, as he'd got his dinner all stirred up in the glue-pot, through being too busy inventing to notice things.

By the time she came back the Professor had got the invention none too securely packed into the box with the two old hats, which, quite by accident, made it fairly snug and not too likely to rattle, and nearly tied up in some paper too small for it, and while she was busy tying up the string on one side, the Professor wrote the address on the other side:

> To General Shatterfortz,
> Standeesey Camp,
> Quickmarch Halt,
> Shunbury.

'Shall I run and post it for you, sir, while you get on with your egg?' asked Mrs Flittersnoop.

'Er – yes, yes, thank you,' said the Professor. So Mrs Flittersnoop put on her hat and went rather slowly to the Post Office, which was her idea of running, while the Professor drank his tea straight out of the pot and wondered why he didn't care much for it, which was his idea of getting on with his egg. But he was thinking about a letter which he had to write and which it was rather drastically vital should reach the General at the same time as the parcel.

'Dear General,' he wrote, 'I am sending you my latest invention. It is an entirely new kind of bomb . . .'

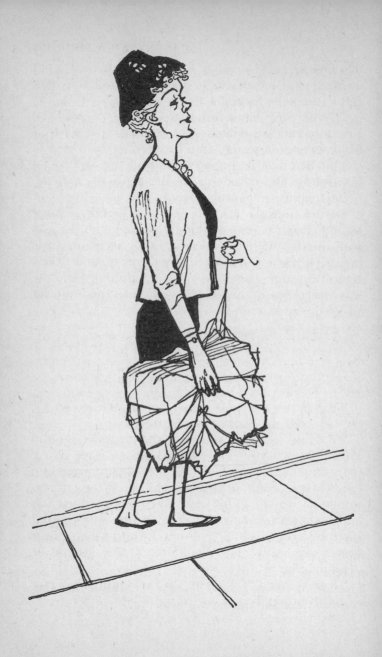

Then he went on to explain all about how the bomb worked, which used up all the writing paper he had and most of the wrapping-up paper left over from the parcel, not to mention three sides of the hardly cardboard and almost no longer boxes, plus the back of last week's calendar with a corner missing.

The Professor had just finished his letter when Colonel Dedshott of the Catapult Cavaliers arrived.

'Ah! Dedshott,' said the Professor, 'I have just completed a new invention that will change all our ideas of soldiering. Let me explain it to you. Or no, wait a minute. Here is a description of it that I have just been writing. You can read that.'

'Ha! ta,' said the Colonel, who'd had so many of his ideas on all sorts of things changed so many times by the Professor's inventions that he wasn't at all sure what some of his ideas were by now, if they were anything. And as for his own profession, the Colonel's idea of that was no end of soldiers, plenty of brass buttons and swords and guns, a big field, a nice sunny day, and 'Shun, left, right, halt, fire, advance – retire, jump to it – as you were, bing bang, step a pace to the rear and do up that button, rat-a-tat, bang, boom, crash.' Enemy routed. War over. Flags, bands, cheers, and plenty of medals for everyone. And a rather nice sort of idea he thought it was, so he took the Professor's exceedingly wholesale letter and began to read it, although not intending to make any difference to things.

The Professor had got things a bit fuddled up as usual. There was no page three at all. Page nine came immediately before page five. There were four page sevens, one of them blank, and quite a portion of the description was in several foreign languages that the Professor liked showing off about.

'Ha! wonderful. Most clever! Astounding, what!' said the Colonel, handing the letter back to the Professor, who stuffed it into an envelope and put it in his pocket so as not to forget to post it.

'The bombs,' cried the Professor, beginning to scatter his five pairs of spectacles about, which he always did when he got excited, 'can be thrown by hand, fired from cannons, dropped from aeroplanes, left about by battleships, or sent flying through the air all by themselves and steered about from the ground so that they drop anywhere you like. They can,' he finished, clapping all his pairs of spectacles on at once, some of them upside-down, 'be made to go off either in one big – er – bang or in several successive smaller, but – er – um – extremely noisy – er – bang-ettes.'

'Astounding!' gasped the Colonel, who had thought that the invention was a new sort of idea for making sergeant-majors' tea in extra large quantities.

'I have sent my first model to General Shatterfortz,' said the Professor. 'If he approves of it I shall expect – er – great things.'

Two days later Professor Branestawm and Colonel Dedshott met again, and that reminded the Professor. 'Oh, my goodness gracious me! Oh dear, dear!' He suddenly started jumping about and waving his hands which he had put into his pockets to get his walking-about spectacles.

'The letter!' gasped the Professor. 'I forgot to post the letter that explains my new bomb!'

'Post it now,' growled the Colonel, who wanted to get home to his supper.

'No, no, too late!' cried the Professor. 'They won't

understand my bomb without the letter or my letter
without the bomb. You don't understand, Dedshott.
This is my greatest triumph of invention. I dare not
risk things not being understood. Besides' – he ran his
hands through what little hair he had, which was so
little as to make the running of hands through it
nearly impossible – 'the General will not know who
sent the invention or whose it is. Somebody may steal
the model. Anything may happen. Oh, oh dear me!
why are we Professors so given to forgetting things?'

There was no answer to the question, partly because
it wasn't the sort of question one does answer, but
mostly because they'd arrived at the Colonel's house,
and out of it, the moment they arrived, came a most
unexpected crowd of soldiers, who swarmed round
Colonel Dedshott and carried him off, protesting like
anything.

'Oh! dear, dear, most awkward,' and the Professor
began to run after them, but gave it up after about a
yard and three-quarters because both his boots fell
off as he'd forgotten to fasten them, though they were
all right for walking along in if you didn't mind not
picking your feet up.

'Um, tut, tut!' said the Professor, 'there goes Dedshott, carted off by a lot of his military friends.
Regimental sort of dinner or something, I suppose,
though it seems rather late in the evening for that kind
of thing. Oh! I must telephone to the General. Yes,
that's what I must do. Yes. Now, I must be very busi-
ness-like and everything will be all right.'

But, of course, everything was anything else but all
right. The Professor ran to the nearest telephone place
with his boots in his hand, but pressed the button too
soon and lost the only two pennies he had with him.

He tried again with four halfpennies and then with a button and a medal off his watch chain, that he had won at school for algebra or something, but the telephone didn't take kindly to medals or halfpence or buttons unless they were marked 'A' or 'B', which those weren't, and it shot them out again with a bit of a clang onto the floor.

'This is terrible!' gasped the Professor. He dashed out of the telephone place, leaving his boots behind, where they were found next day by a rather smart young lady who sent them to a hospital, but the Chief Doctor's dog got at them, so they were more or less wasted. Fortunately, the road to the Professor's house from the telephone place was smoothish, so he got there with only his socks worn out and not his feet as well. Then, putting on his slippers, he rushed off to the station, found the last train had gone, slept between two rows of milk churns, and managed, eventually, to get to the General's Headquarters rather early next morning, considerably before even a soldier's breakfast time, which is so early as to be almost in the middle of the night, but not quite.

'Excuse me, can you tell me where the General lives?' asked the Professor of a spare soldier who seemed to have been left out all night.

'Halt, who goes there?' said the soldier, bringing his rifle and bayonet clickety clank within an inch of the Professor's nose. Then suddenly he dropped his rifle and leapt at the Professor.

'Professor Branestawm, sir, of-all-people-well-now!' he cried. It was Mrs Flittersnoop's sister Aggie's cousin's young man!

Of course that made things easier, because he soon called some other spare soldiers and they took the

Professor along to the General's office kind of tent sort of place. But on the way a little clump of very brisk soldiers suddenly swung round a corner, left, right, left, right, looking straight ahead. And oh! good gracious, in the middle of them was Colonel Dedshott with no coat on! And a wild look in his eyes.

'Dedshott!' cried the Professor.

'I – I – Branestawm,' cried the Colonel. But the brisk soldiers wouldn't let him stop. They rattled him on in a fearful hurry and swept the Professor out of the way so swiftly that he sat down in a puddle – though happily it was a dried-up one.

'Bless me, whatever are things coming to?' gasped the Professor. 'Are those friends of Dedshott's, or what?'

'Shot at dawn,' said one of the spare soldiers, lighting a very stumpy little cigarette without scorching his nose, goodness know how.

'What!' cried the Professor.

'Shot at dawn,' said the soldier. 'He sent a bomb to the General, but they nabbed him. Left his address on the paper. Silly chump. Serve him right. Let him blow up the General if he wants to, but what about us is what I say.'

The Professor disappeared in a cloud of dust in the direction of the General's tent. The General was in bed snoring like someone sawing wood in a tin shed. The Professor rushed forward to wake him up, caught his foot in no end of ropes, and the whole tent came down on top of them. Arms and legs and bits of tent and professorish spectacles and a General's whiskers waved about in the wind. Splutterings and commands and muffled noises came out of the muddle. The General's soldier-servant arrived with hot water in an old tin and hurriedly went away again, thinking he'd better pretend he hadn't seen anything, because the army is so strict about everything.

Outside the camp, Colonel Dedshott stood with his back to a wall with a row of very nervous soldiers in front of him. He was going to be shot for sending a bomb to the General. But he hadn't sent any bombs to anyone. He'd said so forty-nine times, but they wouldn't believe him. Oh, oh, oh! it was the Professor who had sent the bomb and forgotten to send the letter saying it was a model. And he'd wrapped it in a piece of paper something had been sent to Colonel Dedshott in and which the Colonel had brought him round something else in. Nobody knew the bomb was a model. They tried the Colonel very rapidly, military fashion, asked him millions of questions and wouldn't let him answer any of them and here he was. Going to be shot. Oo-er! Poor old Dedshott. Terrible! Awful!

An officer rapped out a command and the soldiers raised their rifles.

'Stop, I tell you,' shouted the Colonel, frantically. 'It's all wrong. I didn't send a bomb. There's a mistake. Let me find things out. I – I what – stop – I –'

His words were drowned in a terrific but ragged sort of many bangs as the soldiers let off their rifles, and the Colonel fell to the ground just as the Professor and the General dashed up, the General still in his pyjamas and the Professor still in most of the tent.

'Too late, too late, what!' panted the General.

Then a most surprising thing happened. Colonel Dedshott got up. Yes, he did and all.

'Branestawm!' he cried, rushing forward. 'Thank goodness you've come, what!'

'Have the goodness to explain, sir,' bristled the General, starting to be all fierce again now that the Colonel wasn't shot, and trying to be extra fierce to make up for being in his pyjamas, which he felt looked a bit silly. 'Have the goodness to explain how you come to be alive after being shot at dawn. Don't you know the rules and regulations?'

'Branestawm's bullet-proof vest,' said the Colonel, opening his shirt and revealing a very knitted-up sort of arrangement of metal that he had on underneath. 'The Professor invented it ages ago and left it at my house and I always wear it in case of accidents.'

Then there was plenty of talking and waving of arms about while the Professor managed to explain about the bomb. But the General wouldn't have believed him and would probably have had them both shot at the next dawn, with cannons or something, to make sure, only the Professor was able to show him that the bomb he had sent didn't have any bangy stuff inside, so couldn't have been intended to blow him up. So that settled things, and as soon as the General could get himself properly dressed, which took a bit of a time because Generals are a bit on the elaborate side, they all had a very military sort of breakfast of bacon pudding and tea with far too much sugar in it, drunk out of tin mugs.

Colonel Dedshott was given an entire battalion of soldiers to drill up and down and play about with to make up for being almost shot at dawn by mistake, and both he and the Professor stayed a few days at the camp by way of a holiday, which they both felt they deserved.

14

To Please Mrs Flittersnoop

MRS FLITTERSNOOP, Professor Branestawm's house-keeper, was never a one to complain, as she would have told you herself. In fact, she had been telling the Professor so for weeks and weeks.

No, Mrs Flittersnoop was never a one to complain. 'But really, sir, if I might make so bold as to say so,' she said, 'what with this hot weather and the extra rooms that have been built on to the house, and your new Inventory on the roof, sir, not to mention the way people do take to popping in to see you at all hours, sir, I'm not saying that I couldn't do with a bit of help now and then.'

'Oh – ah – um, yes, of course!' said the Professor, closing all his five pairs of spectacles together with a rattle, 'of course. Your sister from Lower Pagwell, Mrs Flittersnoop. By all means, or if the apex of the triangle ABC bisect the line DE with a temperature of –'

'It wasn't my sister Aggie I was thinking of, thank you all the same, I'm sure, sir,' said Mrs Flittersnoop, dropping a tea tray rather clangishly to stop the Professor going off into scientific thoughts again.

'Um – a – ah, I see!' said the Professor, who didn't see at all. 'You have another cousin, perhaps, or an auntie. Ask them up by all means.'

'Thank you, sir, but it's these labour-saving things I was thinking of, sir, if you don't mind my saying so. They do bring out some wonderful machines for letting you go to the pictures on washing day, or so the advertisements say. Not that you can believe all they tell you in advertisements and not that I was ever much of a one for the pictures, but –'

She got no further. The word machines had set the Professor off in the most non-stoppable way.

'Um – ah! yes, machines, let me see,' he said. 'What sort of machines? To do what sort of things? How about a machine for making cups of tea –?' He was three parts of the way through an explanation of his idea of a machine like that, with numbered buttons to press according to how many lumps of sugar you took, and a lever to pull if you wanted China tea, when Mrs Flittersnoop managed to stop him and do a bit of explaining herself, which made the Professor's head go round for a change.

At last, after some very mixed up sort of conversation and plenty of waving of hands and a great deal of domestic-sounding talk from Mrs Flittersnoop and no end of scientific sort of exclamations from the Professor, they managed to decide how many hoped-to-be-labour-saving inventions could be done with about the house. Then the Professor went into his Inventory to start inventing and Mrs Flittersnoop went down to her sister Aggie at Lower Pagwell, partly to tell her all about things and partly to get out of the way in case the Professor's inventing caused any drastic, sensational or collapsible kinds of uproar, which it was rather pobably likely to do.

For weeks and weeks the Professor stayed in his Inventory, only popping out now and then to say, 'Mrs Flittersnoop, have you seen the small screwdriver?' and 'Mrs Flittersnoop, will you go out and get me some long nails,' and 'Mrs Flittersnoop, come and show me what goes on the table first when you lay tea,' and 'Mrs Flittersnoop, can you hold this while I fix a spring to it?'

The first few times there was no reply, because Mrs Flittersnoop was still at her sister Aggie's, where she'd finished telling her about the Professor and was being told about her sister Aggie's little girl's hair that wouldn't go curly, not though they put it in papers every night and gave her burnt crusts for breakfast every morning. But after a bit Mrs Flittersnoop began to think she'd rather be possibly blown to bits over the Professor's inventions than absolutely certainly talked to bits over her sister Aggie's little girl's uncurlable hair. So she went back just in time to see the small screwdriver being run away with by the next door cat. Then she got things, and showed him this and that, and held one thing and another. And she took the Professor his meals into his Inventory, as he couldn't stop to come out for them, and several times he invented them into his inventions instead of eating them.

Then one frantic Friday, when the baker left a large brown loaf instead of a small one, and the milkman didn't come the second time, and the laundry sent back one of the best tablecloths with a teeny hole in it marked round with a terrific circle of red cotton, which was their way of saying they hadn't done it – the Professor came bursting out of his Inventory with pairs of spectacles hung precariously on all parts of him and his mouth full of screws.

'Success! Magnificent success!' cried the Professor, trying to put a handful of screws on his nose in mistake for one of his pairs of spectacles and letting them trickle down all over his face. 'Mrs Flittersnoop, I have altered all our ideas of housework. My inventions will make housekeeping a game. I will demonstrate them to you.'

'Indeed, sir, that's very good, I'm sure,' said Mrs Flittersnoop, who felt that her ideas of housekeeping could do with some altering and who found housekeeping for the Professor rather a game as it was.

'There you are,' said the Professor proudly. He pointed to a row of the most uncalled-for-looking arrangements. They were his housework-doing machines, and they consisted of:

1. A Washing-up Machine with detachable soap shaker and a knob which, when twiddled, caused the machine to dry up the crockery it had just washed up.
2. A Bed-making Machine, adjustable for single and double bed and complete with pillow-case putting-on gear.
3. A Window-cleaning Machine, arranged to crawl up the walls to do the outsides and wipe its wheels carefully on the mat before coming in to do the insides.
4. A Ceiling-dusting Machine, with rotary cobweb eradicator.
5. A Table-laying Machine, fitted with different coloured buttons to be pressed according to what meal was to be laid. The Professor was determined to have coloured buttons on something. A special lever for Breakfast-in-bed. This machine could also be reversed for clearing away again after meals.
6. A Stair-rod Polishing Machine.

7. A Fire-laying-and-lighting Machine, with automatic coal smasher, coke buster, oscillating poker, and cinder disposer.
8. A Floor-polishing Machine, with rug-shaking attachment fitted with a string to be wound-up or let-out according to the pattern of the rug to be shaken.

There was also a detector for finding out where the marmalade had been put, as Mrs Flittersnoop often put it in different places, and a highly elaborate and nowhere near understandable device for making used matches strikeable again.

'Well, I do think that's nice, that I do, sir,' said Mrs Flittersnoop. She very gingerly tried the Washing-up Machine on the dinner things. 'Zim-zim-zum, clankety splosh whiz-whir.' All done!

'There now,' she cried, and turned on the Table-laying Machine with the 'Tea' button pressed. 'Popetty-pip, swish, clink, tinkle.' Tea laid!

'Well, I never, that I'm sure, sir!' she exclaimed, coming over all delighted.

'Look at this one,' shouted the Professor from upstairs, where he'd unmade the beds and made them again ten times with his machine.

The machines were most successful. All except the Marmalade Detector, which would keep finding the lemon cheese and the apricot jam instead, possibly as they were something like the same colour. But what was that to worry one, with all the housework getting itself done, clankety-popetty-chug-a-chug-zim? What indeed? The Professor's house resounded with mechanical noises. Everywhere shone and sparkled. The place was almost uncomfortably clean. The meals

were ready with slightly troublesome regularity
because the Professor hardly even managed to be ready
for a meal at the exact moment that Mrs Flittersnoop
and the machines had it ready for him. The windows
were so clean that people living two streets away could
almost see the pattern on the wallpaper. The stair
rods glittered. The toast rack was completely crumb-
less. You could have eaten off the ceiling if it hadn't
been too much of an upside down thing to do. And as
for the floors, they were most drastically hygienic.

Professor Branestawm went round to his friend
Colonel Dedshott of the Catapult Cavaliers, to tell
him about the machines and he made the Colonel's
head go round and round so rapidly, explaining everything at once, that he had to put his hat on even though
he was indoors.

'I must make you some machines, Dedshott,' said
the Professor. 'You'll be surprised. Alter all your ideas
of housework. They will make housekeeping a game,'
he said.

'Ha! very clever, Branestawm, you know what!'
said the Colonel, whose idea of housework was to let
his two ex-Catapult Cavalier Butlers do it by numbers.
'No use to me, though. Not enough work here. Manage
very well, what! House clean as new pin, dash it!'

'Um!' grunted the Professor. 'Well, what about a
cup of tea?'

And as he said the words a cup and saucer landed in
the front garden and smashed to bits on a pink stone
rabbit the Colonel's step-cousin had given him.

'Good gracious!' cried the Professor. 'That looks
like one of my cups and saucers. I recognize the pattern. Doesn't match. Invented it myself.' He dashed
out just in time to catch a sugar basin, while the

Colonel following close behind received a bread-and-butter plate on the head and a milk jug on his foot.

'Table-laying Machine!' gasped the Professor. 'Or else Washing-up Machine! Control spring must have slipped!'

Crockery was falling in showers in the streets of Great Pagwell as the Professor, still holding the basin, into which his spectacles were falling as he ran, followed by Colonel Dedshott with half a bread-and-butter plate lodged on his very military hat, tore round to the Professor's house, from the windows of which the crockery was being hurled.

'You take front, I'll take rear!' panted the Colonel, coming over rather strategic. The house was more than ever full of automatic noises. But it was no longer even comfortably clean. Everywhere was patent-pandemonium and ultra-uproar and mechanical-muddle.

'Oh dear, good gracious me!' wailed the Professor, dodging a large rug that came hurtling downstairs, wrapped round three-dozen stair rods. 'Mrs Flittersnoop! Mrs Flittersnoop!'

But Mrs Flittersnoop was at the pictures. Lucky for her perhaps.

Crash! Eight glass tumblers, full of coke, were slammed down on the dining-room table and immediately snatched up again and washed in stair-rod polish.

'Help, oh dear, help!' cried the Professor. 'Machines have got mixed up.'

They certainly had. Each machine was trying to do bits of the other machines' jobs. The Floor-polishing and Rug-shaking Machine had shaken the tea-table cloth so vigorously that all the tea-things had gone flying out of the window. The Washing-up Machine had already taken the windows out, washed and dried them, and put them in the china-cupboard. The Table-laying Machine, with all its buttons pressed through hitting the door, was doing its best to lay breakfast, dinner, tea, and supper all at once, using windows instead of crockery and sheets instead of table-cloths. The Fire-lighting Machine had got itself made into the Professor's bed and was filling the pillows with coal. The Marmalade Detector was triumphantly waving about a pot of marmalade it had managed to find at last and the marmalade was flying up and sticking to the ceiling, which was giving the Ceiling-dusting Machine rather a time of it, as marmalade is so much less dust-away-able than cobwebs.

'All right, Branestawm!' shouted Colonel Dedshott, climbing through the scullery window, where he was promptly seized and washed up very thoroughly by the Window-cleaning Machine assisted by the Floor-polishing Machine.

'Pah! dash it, you know,' he spluttered, managing to push the Window-cleaning Machine into the kitchen fireplace, where it began to sweep the chimney with a wash-leather. 'Confound your inventions, Branestawm. Look at me!'

But the Professor couldn't look at anyone. He was completely enveloped in four table-cloths, two eiderdowns, and a yard and a half of stair carpet with the Ceiling-dusting Machine, which had given up the marmalade as a bad job, on top of him, busily making used matches strikeable and putting them in the toast rack.

With grunts and growls the Colonel got the Professor untangled just as four of the machines began a twisted-together and inside-out sort of bed-making on

the stairs with three rugs, a teapot, an old coat of Mrs Flittersnoop's, a yesterday's currant cake, and seven roller towels, while the Marmalade Detector, having used up all the marmalade on the ceiling, was rapidly sprinkling honey, golden syrup, and yellow plum jam over the bathroom.

'Oh, my goodness! Oh, good gracious! Oh, bless me, why do I keep inventing things like this?' spluttered the Professor.

Mrs Flittersnoop came back from the pictures, gave one look and three screams, and went back to her sister Aggie's. Bang, thud, zim-a-zim, splosh! 'Bless me!' Poppety-slam. 'Confound the thing, what!' Ziz-ziz-clank. 'Pah!' Wow!

The Professor managed to twiddle some knobs and pull some levers which put the Window-cleaning and Ceiling-dusting Machines out of action. Gradually they got the upper-hand. Gradually the mechanical tumult died down.

The Colonel sank wearily on to the Professor's bed and instantly had his pockets filled with coal by the Fire-lighting Machine that was still there.

At last all the machines were either stopped or smashed or otherwise dealt with and the Professor and the Colonel went to the Colonel's house for plenty of hot baths, and the Professor put on an old uniform of the Colonel's while his own clothes were cleaned, but didn't look any more rum than usual because it was impossible.

'My Housekeeping Machines are very clever, though I say it myself,' said the Professor some time later, after Mrs Flittersnoop had had her sister Aggie and her cousin Kate and her Auntie Helen and her friend

Fannie Fussfat along to help get the Professor's house un-mechanically cleaned up with quite un-scientific brooms and brushes and mops. 'I have therefore presented them as an – er – as a special exhibit to West Pagwell Technical Institute Museum,' he went on, 'they should prove most instructive.'

That week, all the Pagwell newspapers printed photos of the machines with a little note under them, saying: 'Quaint gardening implements discovered by Professor Ramskorn and presented by him to West Pagwell Museum.'

And Mrs Flittersnoop had to go on managing as best she could by having her sister Aggie up to give her a hand whenever she felt she needed it, which was often.

Thank goodness, Mrs Flittersnoop was never a one to complain.

About the Author

NORMAN HUNTER writes: 'I was not invented by Professor Branestawm. I was born. In London, 1899, a few years after the other Normans got there. The place has never been the same since and neither have I. The Beckenham County School was given the job of educating me, but I was almost impervious to learning as I preferred to think about theatrical performances and false whiskers rather than Euclidean problems and vulgar fractions. After escaping from school I had a course of all-in wrestling with typewriters and eventually inserted myself into the advertising profession. I now write advertisements of such allure that people buy vast quantities of the most unlikely things before they can stop themselves. I am also a conjuror and managed to let off two hundred performances at Maskelyne and Devants before the Nazis hit it with a bomb. By then I was in Bournemouth, but I came back to London in time to be chased out again by flying bombs, and finished the war living on a motor yacht on the Thames.

It is usual for an author to say that none of his characters is intended to represent any person, living or dead. Well, Professor Branestawm jolly well represents me, so someone told me. So now what? Do I sue myself for libel before the Professor sues me? That's a conjuring trick to which I don't know the solution.'

Other books by Norman Hunter are described overleaf.

The Incredible Adventures of
Professor Branestawm

Norman Hunter

The Professor was a great (if absent-minded) inventor, always ready to turn his genius to the practical affairs of housekeeping, whether in the matter of a burglar trap or some comprehensive device to get spring-cleaning over quickly. His best intentions, however, seemed to land him in the worst scrapes. Sometimes they involved his Housekeeper, Mrs Flittersnoop, sometimes his best friend Colonel Dedshott, but somehow he never managed to solve the comparatively simple problem of keeping count of the five pairs of spectacles which he generally wore simultaneously, so as to be prepared for all eventualities.

The Dribblesome Teapots and
other Incredible Stories

Norman Hunter

'Oh, oh, oh, oh! This is terrible,' cried the Queen. 'Not a teapot in the Palace that can be used. Oh, disgraceful! I must have a teapot that doesn't dribble, I must! I must! Half the kingdom as a reward for anyone who can bring me a teapot that pours without dribbling!'

'Here, here, half a mo!' cried the King, getting all agitated. 'You can't do that. What do you think's going to happen to Sypso-Sweetleigh if you go offering half of it for teapots?' But it was too late, the Royal Herald had shouted the proclamation all round the city.

This is a marvellous collection of outrageous fairy tales, where the characters struggle against problems that are not nearly as simple as the old legends suggest.

The Puffin Book of Magic

Norman Hunter

The magic in this book will not enable you to turn your school teacher into a chocolate cream frog, or cause a mighty palace to arise in the back garden. But it does show you how to perform exciting, amusing, mysterious, and somewhat joyous conjuring tricks, to entertain your friends and cause them to think you no end of a clever chap (or girl of course). It also shows you how to have a bit of fun making some of the things used in the tricks, without also making too much mess.

Norman Hunter, who conjured up the Professor Branestawm stories for you, has included several tricks that he performs in his own Chinese magic act, which he lets off under the name of Ho Wat Fun.

Jill McDonald has waved her magic pen and produced out of her newest hat the delicious illustrations.

MIDNITE

Randolph Stow

Midnite was not very bright and so when he became an orphan his animal friends decided he should be a bush-ranger, but he wasn't very good at that either. He robbed a judge, and Trooper O'Grady robbed him.

A funny and unusual book, for readers of nine and over.